Out

of the

Blue

Out
of the
Blue

a novel

Virginia Young

Riverhaven Books

Out of the Blue is a work of fiction. While the settings of Plymouth, Massachusetts and the surrounding towns are actual, any similarity regarding names, characters, or incidents is entirely coincidental.

Published in the United States by Riverhaven Book, Massachusetts.

ISBN 978-1-937588-40-3

Printed in the United States of America
by Country Press, Lakeville, Massachusetts

Designed by Stephanie Lynn Blackman
Whitman, MA

In Memory Of
Toby

Special thanks to
my daughter for her input throughout this process,
my husband for his technological assistance,
and Christopher and Nicholas for the humor they inspire in my life.

Chapter One

Samantha Elwyn turned her coat collar up and pulled it closer to her slim throat then tucked her hands into the warm, deep pockets of her tan wool coat. It was, she thought, always colder by the water and she wished she'd remembered to bring gloves.

Plymouth Harbor was darkened to the point where only lights reflecting into the water from scattered boats and one lamp on the pier where the Mayflower was docked provided glimpses of sketchy shapes, black masts against a lavender blue sky. It was Thanksgiving Eve and there was something special in the air.

"Hey, Elwyn!" she heard from the direction of the pier's end. She slowed her pace and looked toward the bay. Who, she wondered, would be calling to her and by her last name?

"Elwyn!" she heard again, and then she decided that it had to be someone who knew that she was down from Boston where she lived and worked, spending the holidays with her family in Plymouth. She hesitated then walked toward the light attached to a thick column of wood near to where two or three boats were docked.

As she moved, squinting to see who was calling to her, she saw a tall man walking toward a tethered boat, one used for harbor tours. Two men in dark knitted hats smiled and waved at him, and then they turned their attention to Samantha. With her long chestnut hair she was easy on the eyes, especially beneath the glow of one bright lantern.

"Eldon, my boy," one of the men said to the tall, chestnut haired man, "who's your friend'?"

Samantha found herself staring at someone close to her age who possessed spectacularly good looks and the exact color hair as her own.

"Can't say I know," he said as a reply and with a smile to Samantha.

She was feeling confused. They'd called him Eldon. Maybe they hadn't called out Elwyn after all. "I think," she said, "I may have heard wrong. I thought my name was being called. Sorry." She turned to walk away.

"Your name's Eldon?" he asked.

Samantha stopped and faced him. "It's Elwyn, Samantha Elwyn."

"Oh," he said. "Well these characters on the boat are being wise guys." He reached out, offering his hand as an introduction. "I'm Gray. Nice to meet you, Samantha. Are you from around here?"

Samantha was slow to pull her warm right hand from her pocket but, when she did, she found an even warmer place for it in his firm but gentle grasp. "Not really," she said. "I'm visiting my grandparents for Thanksgiving. But, I'm curious. Why do they call you Eldon if your name is Gray?"

He released her hand reluctantly and smiled. "They're antagonists," he began in a loud voice so that the men could hear. "I have a good mind to fire them both!" Then he moved several feet away from the boat, walking slowly with Samantha toward the street. "They found out that my middle name is Eldon, my mother's maiden name; they think it's funny."

She smiled and nodded. "Is that your boat they're tying up?"

"No, but I'm responsible for it and two others. They belong to an old friend; we run tours in season. Right now they're being overhauled for the winter."

"So you have winters off," she said.

He smiled. "No such luck. I have a job; I'm an architect, but I inherited this job managing three tour boats. The gentleman who owns them hired me when I was a kid and he's not doing too well right now. I'm just giving him a hand."

Samantha turned to look at him. "What do you design?"

"Mostly commercial properties: strip malls, office buildings, and some homes, which is what I prefer. What about you? What's your story?" he asked as he tucked his hands into the pockets of his leather bomber jacket.

"I write children's books and I plan projects and space for kids in a Boston museum."

"Really?" he said. "That sounds like fun."

"It is," she said. "I love it."

They began to walk slowly toward the street again.

"So, you're here for Thanksgiving?"

"Yes, my grandparents live here and they gather us for holidays as best they can. My parents, my brothers - we're all going to be together, which is unusual for us. My parents are both oceanographers, often on a vessel far away, and my twin brothers live in California. So this time together is rare."

Gray looked at her beautiful face and wished he could take note of her eye color. The light nearer to the street was dim; he could not tell if they were blue or green.

"Sounds like a nice reunion," he said.

"I hope so," she said and laughed. "We tend to play Monopoly or Scrabble when we get together and they're all very competitive. Well, nice to meet you. I should get going, with the dark they'll be wondering where I am."

"Have a nice holiday," he said.

She smiled and waved, "You too."

As she walked away, Samantha shuddered, not with the cold but with her thoughts. He's just too darned good looking for me, she decided. One of those guys all the girls drool over: trouble.

She walked across the street and up a slight hill to her grandparents' home. The lights in the house were welcoming and she knew there'd be warm cider inside and the aroma of all sorts of baked goods. After opening and then closing the heavy oak front door she hung her coat in a hallway closet and walked into the kitchen.

"Well you had a nice walk," her mother said as she cut green beans and slivered almonds into a casserole dish.

"Good Lord," her grandmother said, "they were about to send out the Mounties for you! There, Sweetie, cut these apples into nice thin slices for me, will you? I'll go ahead and get the crusts ready for the pies."

Samantha smiled and took the bowl of apples and a paring knife to the table where she sat down across from her mother. She sliced into an apple, spraying its juice onto her hands and the sleeves of her pale green sweater.

"When are we going to hear something about your love life?" her grandmother teased.

Samantha looked across the table to her mother and saw the smile and the wink.

"Someday, Gram," Samantha said as she looked around at the cluttered kitchen. There was enough food prepared to feed an army and more being made. Her grandmother always said she wanted plenty of food so that if someone stopped in to visit they could eat heartily.

Until after ten that evening they were cooking and doing dishes, finally getting the food put away in the refrigerator and pantry and the utensils washed and out of sight. At that point Samantha and her family gathered together with a warm cup of cider, a chat, and the eleven o'clock news before going to bed.

On Thanksgiving morning, the family woke up to the sweet smell of cinnamon rolls and coffee. Samantha smiled as she slid her feet into warm slippers and pulled a pale yellow fleece robe over her pajamas before making her way down the narrow, curved stairway and into the kitchen.

"Hey, Sunshine," her father said as he stood and reached out to grab his daughter's shoulders for a hug. "Happy Thanksgiving!"

Samantha smiled, wished him the same, and walked to where her grandmother stood at the stove. "I hope you haven't been here all night," she teased as she kissed her grandmother's soft cheek.

"No way," the gray haired woman said as she tapped a wooden spoon against the side of a pan holding freshly cooked Butternut squash. "I had a wonderful sleep; nothing like hard work and the expectation for a wonderful day ahead to give a being the best sleep ever. I love this time of year, now until Christmas, it's the best."

"I agree," Samantha said as she poured herself a cup of coffee and sat across from her smiling father.

"This is a wonderful event," he said. "Nothing like coming home for a holiday with the folks you love. And these cinnamon buns," he said, "are as good as ever, Mom."

"Well, I didn't forget how to make them then," the cheerful woman said. "That's always a good thing. At the age of seventy-one, anything can start to go, you know."

Samantha looked at her father and they laughed. "Gram, you're not ever going to get old on us. I don't care what your age is, you're always going to be the best cook and the best grandmother anyone ever had."

Charles Elwyn looked at his daughter and thought what a great girl she was. "I second that, Mom; you're not allowed to grow old."

"Who's growing old?" Peter Elwyn asked as he entered the kitchen, rubbing his sleep tousled hair, followed by his twin, Kyle.

"No one," their father answered. "No one in this family is allowed to grow old."

"Sounds good," Kyle said as he reached for a cinnamon roll.

"What are we doing today, Gram? Do you need us to help with

anything before dinner?" Peter asked. "Kyle and I thought we'd catch the high school football game. What about you, Dad? You and Gramps want to join us?"

"I might," Charles said. "I'll have to get permission from your mother though."

The twins laughed, as did Samantha, just as Mary Elwyn, with her pretty face framed in short dark curls, entered the kitchen.

"Oops," Charles began, "here's the boss now."

Mary Elwyn gave him a stern look. "Now what are you up to, Charles?" She poured herself a cup of coffee then walked to her mother-in-law and placed a hand on the woman's shoulder. "What can I do?" she asked.

Molly Elwyn smiled at her son's wife and told her to sit down with her coffee. "I've got things under control for now," she said. "I'll get you working later; don't worry about that. I'm going to let you and Sam set the table. I hate getting into those low cupboards where I keep my Peony-Rose dishes, and that's the set I want to use this year."

As they all settled into kitchen chairs, Daniel Elwyn walked into the kitchen from outside, carrying a small armful of kindling. "Gramps, let me help you with that," Peter said. "Is there more outside that you want in?"

"Later," Daniel said with a pat to his grandson's arm. "This will be a good start for our before dinner fire. A nice glass of wine, maybe cider for those tea-totalers among us," he said looking at his wife with a wink and a grin.

"Sit your rear quarters down and have a cinnamon roll," she suggested. "There's fresh coffee too, or tea for anyone who would prefer that."

Samantha looked around the table, complete, her entire dear family there. "This is so terrific," she said. "The sun is shining. It's cold outside, warm inside, and these rolls are so delicious, Gram. I need to learn how to make them."

Mary Elwyn took a sip of her coffee then said, "This sure beats how we spent last Thanksgiving, doesn't it Charlie?"

"Sure does," he said. "We were on a ship off the coast of Greenland, eating dried portions of something or another with a crew of twenty-three burly crewmen and scientists. I like this much better."

"What about Christmas?" Samantha asked. "Can we please have you for that as well?"

"You know what?" her father said. "Yes, you can."

Mary Elwyn looked up at her husband. "We can be home for Christmas? What about the proposed trip to Bali?"

"We'll go after the holidays," he said. "I told the vessel's skipper we'd be back after Thanksgiving for the short voyages out around the northwest coast, but we needed to be home for Christmas. We've missed too many with our family. Bali will wait."

Mary looked like she might cry. "Wow," she said, "I think I love you."

Later in the day, with a few more preparations finished, the four men went off to see the noontime football game. Molly Elwyn sat down with a cup of tea and her Christmas cards, a tradition she loved and managed to at least begin every Thanksgiving while the meal cooked and the house was quiet. "Give me an hour," she said to Mary and Samantha. "I'll get a few done; it's fun. I love looking at my cards and writing little notes to friends."

"I haven't sent cards in years," Mary said. "I used to enjoy it too, but being on a vessel so much of the time, it's difficult."

Molly Elwyn looked at her pretty daughter-in-law. "Are you okay with it all? I mean, is it really okay with you to just about live on an ocean-going boat?"

Mary smiled. "I love the work, and I love being close to Charles all the time. But, I'll admit I sometimes long for the embers of a hearth and home. Someday we'll get back to that, the way it was when the kids were small. For now I'm thrilled to be here and to know that Christmas will be spent with all of you as well. I feel sky high!"

Molly Elwyn laughed. "Okay, that's good. Now scoot, the two of you. Go do something you'd like to do."

"I'm going for a walk by the water," Samantha said to her mother. "Any interest?"

Mary Elwyn touched her daughter's cheek. "You're sweet to invite me, but walking by the water loses its luster when you live on a ship. I have a book I've been longing to get into; I think I'll curl up with that for a while. You go ahead. Dress warm; in spite of the sun, it looks cold out there."

"Okay," Samantha said. "I'm heading out for a walk then. I'll see you both in an hour or so. Anything we need, Gram?"

"Oh, you know what? I could use another pint of cream for coffee. I have some, but you never know. I'd rather be safe than sorry. McHenry's store is open today; you could pick it up there."

"I'll do that," Samantha said with a smile, and then she walked down the hall to retrieve her coat, hat, gloves, and enough cash to purchase the cream.

She made her way down the sloping hill toward the harbor and turned left toward the commercial piers and the very blue sea. It made her feel happy to see how many tourists were there to partake in the historic holiday that this day represented. A Japanese family of five stopped her and asked with manageable English if she would take their photo, the harbor in the background. Samantha was pleased to oblige and took three or four snapshots before she smiled and walked on toward the boats, the gliding gulls swooping above her. She thought of Gray and wondered where he was and how he'd be spending his Thanksgiving. He'd asked about her, but she hadn't asked about him. She wondered if that had been rude, thoughtless of her, and wished she'd inquired politely. For all she knew, she thought, he could be married with ten kids. Forget him, she advised herself; he was too good looking anyway.

Samantha walked to the harbor and then out on a length of jetty where the wind whipped at the white capped waves and threw sprinkles of salty sea on the rocks. She checked her watch and discovered that she'd been gone for about forty-five minutes. She needed to pick up that cream at McHenry's store and get back to help with Thanksgiving festivities.

Inside the warm little store she found the cream in a glass refrigerated case and headed toward the cash register.

"Hi there," a man's voice greeted and she turned to see that handsome fellow from the pier, Gray.

"Hi," she said. "Happy Thanksgiving."

"And to you," he said with a smile. "Last minute shopping?" he asked, beckoning to the pint of cream in her hands.

Samantha looked down at the cream and then up at him. "My grandmother always likes to have plenty on hand."

"Green," he said as he looked into her gleaming face.

"What?" she asked with a confused look.

"Your eyes, they're a beautiful sea green. I wondered what color they were. I couldn't see them in the dim light last night."

Samantha could feel her cheeks warm and was embarrassed that they were surely a tell-tale pink.

"By the way," he said, "you said your last name was Elwyn. You aren't related to Dan Elwyn, are you?"

Samantha laughed. "Of course I am. He's my grandfather."

"For crying out loud! He was my history teacher in high school. How is he?"

"He's fine. He, my Dad, and my brothers all went to the football game."

"I thought about going too, but I needed to check on the boats and decided to skip it this year."

Samantha looked at his chiseled features and his amber colored eyes. "Do you live here in Plymouth? Are you with your family for dinner?"

"Yes and yes. I live here, always have except while in college."

"Do you have children?" she asked.

Gray smiled. "No. I think I should get myself a wife first, don't you?"

Samantha blushed again. "Sorry, I shouldn't have asked that question."

Gray looked down at her. "Why not? No harm in asking a question or two."

"I suppose not," she said. "Well, it was nice to see you again. I'd better pay for this and get going."

"Okay," he said, "but any chance I could stop by later and say hello to my old teacher?"

Samantha's heart beat about ten times faster than normal. "Absolutely, my grandfather would love that. Shall I tell him you're coming by, or would you like to surprise him?"

Gray smiled. "You can tell him red-haired John will be stopping by so he'd better save me a piece of pumpkin pie. I think your grandmother makes the best pumpkin pie I've ever had."

"You know my grandmother too? I'm impressed."

"Molly. She's the greatest. I used to get invited to their house for dinner when we were preparing for debates. Your grandmother's a good cook. She makes one mean meatloaf; I loved it."

Samantha smiled. "Well, I guess I don't have to give you the address then."

"I could find my way there blind-folded," he said. "What time is dinner? I'll pop in a couple of hours later."

"Okay, well the game won't be over until after three, so I would think dinner would be around four. Any time after that is fine. Who's cooking at your house?"

"My mother. My father is home making his potent eggnog, and my sister is there with her husband and three year old son making cupcakes. The adults will all be wasted after that eggnog," he said and laughed.

"But not you?" Samantha asked.

"Might be tempted if it weren't for being so enthused about seeing Daniel Elwyn again. Even though we live in the same town, I never see him. I work the boats in the summer months and I'm in my office the rest of the time, or out on the road visiting sites for new construction."

"Well," she began, "they'll be delighted to see you." She added in her heart that she would be glad to see him as well. There was a magnetism about this man, other than his good looks. He was storybook charming, just like the prince with the happy ending.

"Okay, then," he said. "I guess I'll see you later."

"Great, and I'm to say that John is coming by?"

He smiled, a twinkle in his beautiful eyes. "Yup. John Eldon Grayson. In school the teachers knew me as John, but my friends and family have always called me Gray." He smiled again as he saw the amused look on Samantha's face. "That's it, no more names for me; you've heard them all."

Oh no, she thought, I could think of a few others, such as sweetheart, darling, my love. Samantha smiled and said she'd see him later. She paid for the cream and walked out of the small store, thinking that she really needed to get this guy, this hunky guy, off her mind.

Back in her grandmother's aromatic kitchen, Samantha found her mother drinking a cup of black coffee while slicing pineapple next to the deep farmer's sink.

"Have a nice walk?" Mary Elwyn asked.

"Actually, a terrific walk," Samantha said.

"Oh? What's this all about?" her mother asked with a smile, one hand now with a coffee cup in mid-air. "I know that look, Samantha Jane. Who is he?"

Samantha laughed and picked up a piece of the fresh fruit.

"I met him last night on the pier. It was kind of weird: I thought someone was calling out Elwyn but they were calling the name Eldon. That's his middle name and he was being teased by a couple of men who work for him."

"Tell me more, sounds interesting."

"Not much to tell. He introduced himself, we talked a few minutes, and, while at McHenry's for the cream, I ran into him again. He's coming here later."

Mary Elwyn put her coffee cup and the knife she was using for the pineapple down on the counter top. "Not much to tell? Are you kidding me? And he's coming here later."

"Yes," Samantha said as she slipped another piece of pineapple into her mouth. "But to see Gramps. He had him for a history teacher in high school. He just wants to come by to say hello."

Mary smiled and then took a sip of her coffee. "Sure, whatever you say, kiddo."

"What?" Samantha asked.

"Sure he loved your grandfather, everyone did, but I'd bet all the tea in China that he's interested in my little girl."

"Who's interested in what?" Molly Elwyn asked as she entered the kitchen carrying a bouquet of white Chrysanthemums.

"It's nothing," Samantha said as she turned to greet her grandmother. "I met a former student of Gramp's last night and I ran into him again today at McHenry's. He's stopping by later to say hello."

"Oh, good. Anyone I'd know? What's his name?"

"John Grayson," Samantha said, and then she walked to the sink where she washed her hands before working on preparations for the meal.

"John? My goodness, I haven't seen him in years. What a nice boy he was, a real whiz at the debates. And handsome, all the girls were crazy over him. Is he still handsome?"

Samantha laughed. "Oh yeah, I'd say so."

Mary looked at Molly and winked.

"Well," Molly said, "I'm very glad he's stopping by. Since his retirement, I think your grandfather has been quite lonely for his kids. He especially liked John Grayson; the boy literally won the debates for the team; very bright fellow, and about as sweet as they make them."

Mary gave Samantha a sideways glance, noticing that her daughter was quiet and blushing, a soft smile on her ample lips.

"What should I do next, Gram?"

Molly looked around at the food and then at her list. "How about if you take the walnut cake out of the frig. That will free up some room for other things until dinner, and the cake will be fine at room temperature. After that, maybe you could start to retrieve my Peony-Rose dishes; I'd like to have a few of the serving pieces out."

Without hesitation, Samantha removed the cake from the refrigerator and then went to the lower portion of her grandmother's cupboards for the dishes. Carefully, she placed the antique set on the dining room table, leaving them to be arranged later.

When the men came home from the game, animated with having the winning team, they had warm cider and the meal was served.

"That was the best Thanksgiving dinner you've ever made," Daniel said to his wife of fifty-three years.

Molly gave him a smile. "You say that every year, Daniel."

The older man smiled and patted his stomach. "Well, I guess that means you haven't lost your touch."

"Everything was wonderful," Peter said, and the entire family agreed with their own little comments.

"So, will it be Scrabble or Monopoly?" Peter asked.

Kyle groaned. "Oh, no. The shark is swimming around, ready for his attack."

"You're calling me a shark?" Peter said with a smile. "I'm not the one who plays the killer here. So, which will it be?"

"Count me out," Molly said. "I'll be happy listening to you as you hack one another to pieces over a game. I'm doing the dishes so that dessert can be served a bit later with an uncluttered kitchen."

"I'm with you, Molly," Mary said, and then Samantha decided to help as well.

"I sense fear on your part, dear sister," Peter said.

"I can beat you any day," she replied, "and I will later. Right now I'm doing the dishes with Gram and Mom. You four go ahead and beat each other up."

"No problem here," Charles said as he pulled the Monopoly game from the closet. "Dad and I will beat these pups to a pulp."

Mary smiled at her sons and then turned to place the remaining vegetables into plastic storage containers. Between the clanking of the dishes, pots and pans being washed, dried and put away, and the four men loudly proclaiming their victories over one another, the house was filled with the sounds of content, happy people.

When the doorbell rang at six-fifteen, Molly suggested that Samantha greet their visitor. She untied an apron from the waist of her dark green dress and fluffed her hair as she walked down the hallway to the door.

"Hi," he said as he placed a bottle of wine in Samantha's hands and stepped inside at her urging.

Samantha couldn't help but smile, the red tints to his thick hair were gleaming in the lantern light and he looked like he could burst out with Christmas carols. "Hi," she said. "Come on in. We didn't tell Gramp you were coming, but my grandmother knows and she's thrilled."

Gray followed Samantha into the kitchen and dining room area where the men were closing the Monopoly game with a debate over who won what.

When Daniel Elwyn looked up and saw Gray, he had surprise written all over his face, and then a broad smile broke out as he walked toward his former student with a hand extended. "John Grayson, you son of a gun, how are you?"

Gray reached out for the older man's hands and then they hugged. Within moments the rest of the family was introduced and it was explained that Samantha had run into Gray at the pier and then at the store.

"You'll have dessert with us," Daniel invited. "I remember how you used to like to eat, and my Molly, she's the best little cook in the bay."

Gray looked at Molly and smiled. "I recall every morsel," he said. "I'd love to have dessert with you." He glanced at Samantha and, for a moment, she was thinking that he was looking at her as if she were a piece of creamy pie or a rich cake. She smiled then turned to move away and into the kitchen, out of the limelight where obvious interest might be too easily detected. Once there, she uncorked the wine and placed it and a tray of glasses on the table near the array of desserts.

Hardly a word passed between Samantha and Gray while he was there with all of them; so many conversations mingled without her input and she enjoyed just listening. Every now and then her eyes met his and she quickly looked away, busying herself with pouring coffee, tea, or wine. He was an interesting addition to the family; he fit right in she thought.

"Hey," Kyle began, "maybe you'd enjoy a game of Scrabble after dessert." He directed his invitation to Gray. "We always play; its tradition."

Gray smiled at Samantha, remembering how she'd told him that her family was pretty cut-throat about their game playing. "I don't know if I'm up for it with you guys," Gray said. "I've got the feeling that this is a fairly serious affair."

"Now," Peter said, "who told you we were all that serious? Come on, Gray, we'll take it easy on you."

Gray laughed. "Okay, you talked me into it."

"This is where I sit back in a comfortable chair and enjoy a piece of my mother's wonderful walnut cake," Charles Elwyn said. "You boys play Samantha and have your dessert. She'll whip you two," he pointed to his twin sons. "Not so sure about you, Gray, but she'll be gentle, won't you, Honey?"

Samantha laughed. "Maybe," she said.

Gray gave her a challenging look and smiled. "I think I need a piece of that great pumpkin pie first, a little nourishment to reinforce my Scrabble efforts."

"Well, just be prepared for a cheater," Kyle said of his sister. "She uses words we've never heard of half the time."

"I can't help that you majored in hockey instead of the normal academics," she said.

"Oh, that was cruel," Peter said with a low voice. Everyone laughed, including Gray who thought this was going to be a visit filled with fun, and it certainly didn't hurt that beautiful Samantha was sitting directly across from him, licking her luscious lips from the frosting of walnut cake.

After three competitive games, the first two won by Samantha, the last by Gray with a nine-point lead, the twins threw in the towel and decided they were retiring to the TV room to lick their wounds.

Gray helped gather the pieces together to put the game away and then he said that he should probably go home and visit with his sister and her family; they'd be returning to New Hampshire the next day.

Gray shook hands with all the men, giving a special grasp to his former teacher, hugged Molly and thanked her for a wonderful evening, then turned his attention to Mary. "Thank you," he said. "I really enjoyed this."

"We were happy to have you," Mary said. "I hope we'll see you again."

"I hope so too," he said, and then he looked at Samantha who moved toward the front door and the closet where she'd hung his coat.

"This was a very special night," he said. "I loved seeing your grandfather again, and it was pretty nice to see you too. Thank you for allowing me to come by."

"I enjoyed it," she said. "I'm glad you could make it."

Gray hesitated at the open door. "When are you going back to Boston? I'm assuming that since you work there, you live there. Maybe I'm wrong."

"No, you're right. Not until Sunday at the earliest. Mom and

Dad are leaving then also, and my brothers are flying out on Saturday night. Neither of them really likes the cold and Kyle has a girlfriend in California."

"What about you? Are you a sunshine or snow girl?"

"Both," she said. "I love the seasons here in New England. The cold doesn't bother me at all."

"Good," he said. "How about having dinner with me sometime after your family leaves?"

"But I live in Boston," she said.

"I know my way there," he said with a smile, "and I already know that you can find your way here. Come back and visit your grandparents; they'll love it, and I will too."

Samantha looked down at the wide pine floor and then up into his handsome face.

"So, how do we work this out?"

"I'll call you," he said.

Samantha smiled. "Won't you need my telephone number?"

Gray shook his head. "I already have it. When you went for more coffee, your grandmother slipped me this little piece of paper with your name and number on it."

Samantha looked surprised and then she laughed. "Okay, goodnight, Gray."

"Goodnight," he said softly, and then he was gone.

Chapter Two

Back at her apartment in Boston Sunday evening around eight, Samantha was just stepping out of the shower with a large towel draped around her body when the phone rang.

"Hi there," he said.

She knew his voice already. This guy was getting to her and, although very much aglow, she wasn't feeling very secure about that.

"Hi," she said.

"I tried calling at your grandparents' home, but they said you'd left right after your parents did. I was sorry to have missed you. I was going to suggest us having a drink, or coffee."

"That was a nice thought; but I decided that after four days away, it was time to get back to my responsibilities here. I had a great time though. I love Plymouth, and having my family there was a treat."

"I can imagine. My sister, Suzanne, lives in New Hampshire, but it's not more than three hours for her to come down or us to go up, so we see her fairly often. My mother and father need that grandchild fix, can't go more than a couple of weeks without seeing Michael."

Samantha smiled and sat down at one end of her tan chenille sofa, pushing a cranberry colored pillow aside. "I'm sure he's cute. Did you say he's three?"

"Three, nearly four. He's quite the kid, very aware of everything, doesn't miss a trick."

Samantha laughed. "They're amazing at that age, but grown-ups need to watch what they say every minute. They're like little sponges. I come into contact with children that age all the time at the museum. Sometimes I go there to observe, just to kind of take in how they're enjoying my set-ups. If you want an honest opinion, ask a child."

Gray smiled and sat down on a stool in the kitchen. "How long have you been at this museum work?"

"Three years; I was initially asked to design a room based on one of my books, but then they invited me to stay on to continue the development of other projects. I end up there about three days a week; the rest of the time I make good friends with my computer for my writing."

"When does your social life have a space?"

Samantha frowned and was glad he couldn't see her. "That's challenging sometimes, but I manage."

"In what way? Is there a boyfriend in this picture?"

She hesitated, not wanting to admit that there wasn't, but not wanting to lie and say that there was. "No, not really."

"I always wonder what 'not really' means," Gray said with a hint of teasing in his voice.

"I have no idea," Samantha said and laughed. "I think I use that phrase when I'm not feeling too sure of myself."

"Of anyone I've met in at least recent years, you strike me as being *very* sure of yourself. I have the impression that you're very put together."

"Well then, maybe I should have gone in for an acting career," she said smiling.

"Are you kidding me? Do you not feel secure in yourself? If not, you should, you've got it going."

Samantha laughed. "Thanks. I think I've got it together as well as, if not better, than most of my friends, but I still have my doubting moments. Don't you?"

Gray moved from a stool to a roomy chair in the dining area where he had a view of the harbor. "I suppose there are times when I'm not all that sure about things. However, I'm sure about this: I'd like to invite you out for dinner. This is Sunday; I was wondering how Wednesday evening looks for you. Or, if you might be spending a couple of days down here again soon, we could do dinner in Plymouth; the North Star has great seafood."

Samantha squirmed and tucked the soft cranberry pillow under her right arm. "I have no plans to go to Plymouth this coming weekend, but I do go there often. We could wait until I go down there if you'd prefer."

"No," he said, "I'd prefer to have dinner with you this week. Is Wednesday okay with you if I pop into Boston, maybe around seven?"

"Okay. Would you like to come here to my place, or should I

meet you?"

"A gentleman always picks the lady up," he said in a husky voice.

Samantha could visualize him smiling as she was. "Okay, then. Are you familiar with the area of Suffolk University?"

"Yes, one of my buddies went there. I visited often."

"Okay. I live two blocks west of there, on Atlantic Hill Road. It's a tan colored stone building, number twenty-nine, third floor. Step inside, press the buzzer with my name on it, and I'll open doors for you."

"Sounds uncomplicated enough; and is seven good timing?"

"Seven is fine," she said, feeling a chill from head to toe.

"Okay, seven it is. Do you have a favorite place to dine or should I rely on the North End which is my usual haunt in Boston'?"

"I love Italian food; the North End would be great."

"You've got it. See you Wednesday."

When she placed the portable phone back on its receiver, she left her hand there for a few moments, as if she was still holding onto him. She smiled as she wrapped the towel tighter against her body and then made her way toward her bedroom and her green satin pajamas.

During the first part of the week, Samantha spent time at the museum planning a Christmas room in addition to the already bright decorations. She decided on a theme of festively dressed rabbit families enjoying every aspect of the holiday, from tiny lit trees to fruitcakes rich with acorns, carrots, and cucumber sauce topped with bright red cherries. By Wednesday she was exhilarated and exhausted all at once, but she hadn't forgotten for a moment that she was seeing Gray that evening, and she wondered if part of that adrenaline flow was due to him.

In her apartment as she adorned her ears with dangling garnet stones, the buzzer rang and she asked who it was. Gray's voice replied and she smiled as she pushed a button to allow him through a set of glass doors and up the stairs or to the elevator. He took the stairs.

"Hi there," he said as she opened the door wearing a black dress, her chestnut hair cascading over her shoulders. "These are for you," he said as he placed a small bouquet of white roses in her hands.

"Thank you, they're beautiful," she said as she stepped aside. "Come on in. I need to grab my coat and purse, but first let me put these in water. May I offer you anything? Would you like a glass of wine?"

Gray looked around at the tastefully decorated apartment. "I'm all set," he said, "but thank you. I like your place; it has a nice view of the city too."

"Thanks," she said as she returned from the galley kitchen where she found a vase for the roses. "It's convenient here, but whenever I'm in Plymouth I wonder what took me to the city of Boston. I think you're the lucky one to live there, plenty of nice places to walk and you have the sea at your fingertips."

Gray smiled. "You're not exactly a distance from the sea here."

Samantha grimaced a bit. "It's not the same; this is nice but very commercial. In Plymouth it's more historic and scenic. It's the only place I think of as home. Since my brothers and I were teenagers, Mom and Dad have moved us about to wherever their work took them. Plymouth, more specifically my grandparents' home, was the stability in our lives. I love going there."

"I'm good with that idea. So when will you be back there? If we get a good day, I could take you out on one of the boats."

"In the winter?" she asked.

"In the winter," he confirmed. "The harbor gets icy but rarely frozen over. And if not a good time for a boat ride, there are other things we can do. You come down, we'll figure it out."

Samantha smiled as she slipped her arms into her coat which he held for her.

At the North End, edging by carts filled with sacks of potatoes and a vendor selling hot coffee, they made their way to Tony Como's, a place Gray had frequented over the years when in Boston. "Do you know this place?" he asked.

"No," Samantha said, "I don't, but it certainly smells good in here." They were guided through the door and to a table near the hearth where they shed their coats and ordered wine. With stolen glances at one another, they sat back to enjoy the flickering flames and the gentle buzz of others talking and dishes clanking in the bustling kitchen.

"Did you have business in Boston today?" she asked.

Gray took a sip of his wine. "Yes, seeing you."

Samantha blushed and sat back in her chair. "You say all the right things, don't you?" she teased.

Gray smiled. "I try when it's important."

There he goes again, she thought.

"So, tell me about this room you were working on at the museum."

Samantha placed her glass of wine down and folded her hands in her lap, her eyes gleaming in the candlelight from the table. "It's all about Christmas and rabbits," she said with a smile. "It really came out so great. It's not quite finished, but it will be by Friday."

"Was all of this your idea? It's unique, using rabbits. Most people would probably think bears or deer at this time of year, rabbits for Easter."

Samantha smiled. "I know, I'm a bit twisted I guess. When I did a room for Easter, I had bunnies, but the major theme was horses."

Gray laughed. "How did you incorporate horses into an Easter theme?"

"Oh, it was wonderful. There were horses pulling carts that looked like baskets, and, of course, there were bunnies riding in the baskets. And there were horses showing off their Easter bonnets and, for the males, their Easter berets. It was very fancy; the kids loved it. Every child went home with a chocolate horse - it was a popular theme."

Gray took another sip of his wine and then they ordered their meals. He couldn't help but look at her; she had the qualities of a woman in charge mixed with the joy of a child's animated expressions. She was something.

When the waiter had refilled their glasses with wine, Gray looked at Samantha and smiled.

"What's that look for?" she asked with a returned smile as she reached for her water.

"It's just fun being around you. You're creative; you pluck more from life than most people. You have your own life plus that of all you develop. That's pretty interesting."

Samantha felt like she could cry. Was this someone who actually understood all that she was about? How wonderful would that be? Even her family had pretty much taken for granted all of her creative abilities.

"I have fun," she said, "but I work at it. It's important to me that children find a world filled with good things; there's so much junk that can get in the way."

"I agree completely," he said. "A friend of mine, in fact the guy who attended Suffolk and is now a successful attorney in Rhode Island, had to overcome so much. His parents were divorced and fought constantly over the kids. Not who wanted to take them, but who didn't have time for them. It was a rotten way for kids to grow up, feeling like they were inconvenient."

Samantha frowned. "That's hard. I can't imagine that. Other than being a lawyer, how's he doing?"

"He's doing well. I was best man at his wedding last year and now they're expecting a baby in mid-March. He's the type of guy who understands that what he lived with as a kid was nothing to do with him; it was his parents' errors. He wanted to be a lawyer, he wanted a family, he's always put one hundred percent into what he wanted. He's going nuts buying stuff for the baby; he has no idea yet if it's a boy or a girl, so he's bought footballs, a basketball hoop big enough for Michael Jordan, and then a pink teddy bear and a fairly pricey porcelain doll." Gray laughed. "He's a character, one of the good guys I think."

Samantha was impressed that Gray had such a solid friend. "He sounds like a very forthright person," she said.

"He is. Maybe you'd like to meet him and his wife sometime. Paul and Kate live in Providence in a big old Victorian house, twelve rooms of antique moldings and a fireplace in eight of those rooms. It's amazing. They did most of the painting and fixing up themselves; they're clever people, nice people. I think you'd like them."

She nodded as the waiter arrived with their food and a basket filled with warm rolls.

After their meals they were too full for sweets. Gray suggested a walk and then dessert if they felt like some later.

The lights in the North End were colorful and the general atmosphere was happy, people laughing and shopping for Christmas items in little shops here and there. Before long they found themselves walking near to the water, away from the North End and to where the pungent odor of fish and salt air dominated their senses.

"Do you have to get up early?" Gray asked. "I'm afraid we've walked a distance from the car and I don't want to keep you out later than you'd planned."

"I didn't plan," Samantha said with a smile as they stopped on a large wharf. "It's such a crisp evening; I'm enjoying this. Thank you for inviting me out. I'd probably be sharing a bologna sandwich with my cat if I weren't out with you."

"You have a cat? I didn't see a cat at your place."

"She goes under the bed until she knows someone," Samantha said with a laugh.

"You have no idea how many people do that when I arrive on the scene," Gray said solemnly.

Samantha laughed and then they turned around and walked back toward the North End.

"Are you in the mood for dessert?" he asked as he reached for her hand and looped her arm through his.

"I don't know. I'm still pretty full, but maybe a coffee or something. What about you?"

"I have my heart set on a rum slice back at Como's. Is that okay with you?"

"Sure, sounds good," she said as she enjoyed the feel of his strong arm pressed against her own as they walked.

"What are you working on right now? Something commercial or a house?" she asked.

"Right now, I'm finishing up a medical complex, but after that. I have three houses to design. One in Newton, one in Duxbury, and one in Plymouth. "

"Sounds like you're busy," she said.

Gray smiled as they walked in the dark, splashes of lamp light over their faces every few minutes. "Yup, but I like it that way. I'm very fortunate: people tell others about my work and I end up with all free advertising."

"Do you work with someone else or alone?"

"Alone. I could take on a partner, but right now I like it this way."

Samantha could feel the warmth of his body from her elbow down to her gloved hand and when they reached Tony Como's she was sorry to let go of his arm as he held the door open for her to enter.

They were seated at a small round table in the front window of the restaurant where they ordered their coffees and the rum slice for Gray. When it was placed before him, he asked Samantha to try a bite and she did.

"Would you like to share this? Or have one of your own?" he asked as she licked her lips.

"No, but thank you, it's delicious; maybe another time."

"Oh," he began as he held his fork just inches from his firm mouth, "so you'll grant me another time?"

She blushed. "Maybe," she said and then she smiled.

When they arrived back at her apartment, Samantha invited him in and asked if she could get him anything before he left for home.

"I didn't even ask," she said, "but I assumed you'd be returning to Plymouth tonight."

Gray glanced at his watch. "Yes, I actually have a meeting with the construction crew for the medical center at nine in the morning, so I'd better hit the road. But I had a great time tonight. Thank you for joining me."

"Thank you for inviting me along," she said.

At the door, Gray leaned forward just enough to braise her lips with his own, and then he backed up, looked at her, and leaned forward for a deeper, longer kiss. He kept his hands in his coat pockets, her arms were by her side. They both knew that if they reached for one another, he might not be returning to Plymouth that night.

When he had gone, Samantha's white and gray cat came out of the bedroom and sat, watching Samantha hang her coat and tuck her shoes into the hall closet. In the bedroom where she slipped out of her black dress and into a long-sleeved purple satin night gown, she reflected on the evening. It was not like anything she'd ever done before on a date. When she'd been with Jim, they'd always gone to the theatre or to the Pops, nothing that was casual and gave them time to talk. Maybe that's why she hadn't felt bonded to Jim, as nice as he was. He simply didn't have much to say, except about his work as an auditor for the state of Massachusetts. She shook her head, recalling how often she'd felt bored, but listened politely. Gray was far from boring. He was interesting and caring, and he was fun.

When the telephone rang, she expected it might be one of her parents calling from the Canadian coastline before boarding a ship for the next three weeks of work.

"Hello?" she answered the phone.

"Hi." he said.

"Gray?"

"I have to admit it, it's me."

Samantha smiled and sat down on her bed. "Are you all right? Did you forget something?"

"Yes, I forgot that I'd be lonely all the way home."

Samantha laughed. "I see. So you decided to pester me and talk all the way to Plymouth?"

"Oh, I wouldn't do that. I'll let you talk too." He smiled in the shadowy green light reflecting from his dashboard.

Samantha laughed again. "You know, if they ever decide we can't use cell phones while driving our cars, some of us are going to be in trouble."

Gray smiled. "I just about never use mine except to make appointments. I'm actually one of those who would prefer that no one used cells while driving. But there's almost no traffic at eleven on a Wednesday night, so here I am. Am I keeping you from something?"

"Just sleep," she said smiling and petting her cat.

"Would it be unkind of me to keep you on the phone?"

Samantha shifted back against her pillows. "No. I'm comfortable and not all that tired, so talk away."

"Tell me what you liked best about tonight," he said.

Samantha smiled at the question. "Hmmm," she began, "I guess coming home to Lucy, my cat, and having her smile at me as she watched me hang up my coat."

Gray made a pouty face and was glad she couldn't see. "Great, the cat's on a higher level than me. Thanks."

Samantha rolled over onto her stomach and smiled. "Well, she's a very cute cat, you know. But seriously, I loved the entire evening. It was very relaxing, one of the nicest times I've had. Thank you again. What about you? Did you have a best thing tonight?"

He thought about telling her that it was simply being with her, but he didn't want to rush anything and scare her away. "It was all good," he said, "but the way we could talk, that was pretty nice. It felt like we'd known one another for a long time."

Samantha was thinking the same thing. "Could I ask you a personal question?" she said.

"Go ahead," he said as he maneuvered the car onto the Southeast Expressway.

"When is your birthday?"

"Are you into astrology?" he asked.

Samantha laughed. "No, I have no knowledge of it, but for some reason, it's something I like to know about my friends. You don't have to tell me if you don't want to."

Gray smiled as he drove. "It's December second."

"Oh, my gosh, next week."

"So when's yours?"

"Mine's gone by, October."

"October what?" he asked.

"You're going to laugh if I tell you."

Gray started laughing without her answer. "It's Halloween, isn't it?"

Samantha smiled. "Yes, but I am not a witch and I always loved that it came on Halloween; it felt like it was a big party being celebrated just for me."

Gray smiled. "Even your name, like the old TV show, *Bewitched*."

Samantha smiled. "That's not where it came from, but, yes, I recall that show."

"Where did the name come from then, just something your parents liked? It's a pretty name, although I'm very tempted to call you Sam."

"My grandparents tend to call me Sam. But the name came from, well, never mind, you've already had a good laugh at my expense."

Gray chuckled softly and hoped she didn't hear. "Tell me," he said. "Were you named for some infamous relative?"

Samantha grimaced and said, "I was named for my mother's hamster."

Gray laughed so hard he had moisture form in his eyes and then Samantha began to laugh. "I'm glad you're so amused. But there's this: my mother adored that hamster."

"Obviously," Gray said as he wiped his eyes with the back of his hand.

"And you," she began, "did you get your first name from someone in the family?"

"John is pretty generic," he said, "but there were men named John on both sides. For whatever reason, my dad started to call me Gray and it stuck. The teachers in school used John because it was on my records, but half the time when they called on me, I didn't reply because I felt like Gray. Names are a little strange I guess. But, I will admit, I've never known anyone before who was named for a hamster."

"Very funny," she said as she smiled and rolled over onto her back, the cat scampering to avoid being flattened.

"Sam," he said, the one syllable coming so softly from his lips, nearly taking her breath away, "the hamster is one lucky little creature to have had you for a namesake."

"Yes," she agreed, "I'm sure he's been sitting up on a lofty, tiny cloud for many years now, looking down and smiling because I was named for him."

Gray laughed. "Him?"

"Yes, well my mother thought it was a girl hamster, but when it got bigger, she could see that it was a boy hamster. She left the name the same."

Gray laughed again, glad that she couldn't see the pools of liquid coming from his eyes. "I love it," he said. "This is definitely the kind of thing you tell your grandkids someday."

Samantha grimaced. "I'll have to see about that. Where are you at this point?"

"I'm just approaching Hanover; another twenty minutes and I'll be home. But," he said looking at the clock on the dashboard, "it's eleven-thirty. I'm going to let you go to bed and I hope we'll talk soon."

"Okay," she began, "drive safely. Goodnight."

"Goodnight, Sam."

She clicked the off button on the phone and lay there on her bed smiling. He was a charmer, and she'd never laughed so much in her life. Then she thought about being named for a hamster. She'd never revealed that to anyone before. Even though she thought that hamsters were perfectly fine little creatures, couldn't they have named her after some Greek goddess or something?

Without crawling beneath the covers of her bed, Samantha fell asleep thinking about Gray. Everything was telling her that she should beware, that this man was too good to be true. But he was so appealing that he was just about impossible to resist. She had never been a risk taker; this was all new to her, like being washed away in a rip tide to some magical sea where everything was right. She hoped.

In the morning, the skies were dotted with clouds but the sun was pushing itself above, below, and around them, making itself important to the day. Samantha stretched and found her cat curled up at her bare feet and then up greeting her mistress with a wet nose to Samantha's arm. She spoke softly to the cat and then swung her legs out of bed and her feet into slippers. A quick trip to the kitchen to flip on the coffee machine, and then she headed for the bathroom for a quick shower.

Every move she made, her thoughts were of Gray. Had it all been real? Did they have this wonderful evening in the North End and then that on-going conversation, even on his way home? Yes, they had, and it was incredibly perfect. She could barely wait to hear from him again and hoped she would. And then she remembered his birthday was just around the corner. It would be an excellent excuse to see him again. She would find him a gift. She would go to

Plymouth. She would surprise him.

Samantha ran a brush through her long hair and slipped into jeans and a dark blue jersey. She would be working at the museum, putting final touches to the Christmas designs, and then she would be home to work on her latest children's book, a tale about a cow and a deer who became best friends, even though parted by a strong fence. She loved her work and, in fact, decided that it didn't feel like work at all.

As she was about to leave her apartment for the museum, the phone rang and this time it was her mother.

"Samantha, I'm so glad I caught you before you left for work. We're about to get on the ship and you know how those phone systems are, sometimes they're impossible to hear on. I called you last evening, but there was no answer. I talked to Peter and Kyle, so I wanted to connect with you before we go out. Is everything okay? You aren't normally out on weeknights."

Samantha smiled. Even though she was twenty-eight, they worried about her. "I'm fine, Mom. I was out for the evening with that fellow from Plymouth, John Grayson."

"Oh, you were! Wow, that was fast. Good going, Honey; he's adorable."

Samantha smiled. "Yes, well I'm sure that other females have eyes too, so let's not get carried away with this."

"Phooey," Mary Elwyn said. "Go ahead and get carried away; he's worth it."

"Mother," Samantha began, "what are you suggesting?"

Mary Elwyn laughed. "He's pretty darn cute, that's all."

"Yeah, well, that's nice but, fortunately, I'm grounded with my work and my book. You'd love the Christmas room I've designed; it's great. And I'm so elated that you and Dad are going to be home for Christmas this year. I hope you can manage this every year from now on."

"I hope so too, Honey. I love being with all of you so much. Your father and I have talked about it since Thanksgiving and we're really going to try to have holidays at home. We miss all of you, and what's so important out on that ocean that it can't wait? After all, most of what we do concerns sources that have been out there for time eternal."

"Right," Samantha said, "it will be there when you get to it. How's Dad? Is he around? Could I say goodbye to him?"

"He's actually down in the chart room, Honey. We're leaving in minutes, so I kind of doubt he'll get up here to the phone. Could I give him a message?"

"Just to have a safe voyage," she said. "I'm sorry I missed your call last night."

"That's okay. Dad and I want you to have a happy life and it sounds like you had a very nice time with John Grayson. It was fun having him come by at Thanksgiving. Make sure you invite him at Christmas; you know Gramps would love having him again."

Samantha smiled and thought that Gramps was not the only one who would like Gray to stop by, at Christmas or any time. "I'll give that some consideration," she said, knowing full well that she would certainly extend an invitation to Gray for Christmas.

Chapter Three

On Friday of that week Samantha had time at home to work on her latest book, having completed the Christmas room at the museum. She stood at her living room window with a cup of coffee in her hands. Gray was right: the view of the city was great from there. She turned to walk back to her computer when it dawned on her that his birthday, December second, was Sunday. She wanted to give him something meaningful without seeming too clingy. And then she wondered how she would get the gift to him. Should she consider a weekend at her grandparents' home in Plymouth? Would that be pushing too hard? She wasn't sure. She walked to the computer and sat down, deciding to get to work and think about Gray and the gift later.

Early that evening, Julie, her friend and boss at the museum, called and asked if they could meet for dinner. She also wanted to know, if by any chance, Samantha had a copy of her third book, one about the relationship between a unicorn and a butterfly.

"I think I do," Samantha said. "I'll check. Why do you want it?"

"My niece's birthday is coming up; I'm going there for cake and she's so into unicorns. I gave her two of your other books and she loves them; I want her to have the entire collection some day."

Samantha laughed. "There are only eight so far; it shouldn't be difficult to get the others. Anyway, hold on a minute, I'll go check and see what I've got." Samantha placed the phone down and went to her hall closet where she hauled out a carton filled with her books. The unicorn story was there, one of four copies. She walked back to the kitchen area and picked up the telephone. "Julie," she began, "I have it. I'll bring it with me tonight. Where are we eating? I'm starved."

When Samantha arrived back at her apartment after dinner she tossed her coat over a chair and went to the blinking red light on her answering machine. She listened and smiled.

"Hey, Sam," his silky voice came through, "it's Gray. I'm on my way out for a bite to eat and I was thinking about you, wishing you could join me. Since you are obviously out, and Lucy isn't good about answering the phone, I guess we won't connect tonight, but hopefully we will soon. Take care."

She held the phone then pressed the button to hear the message again.

Samantha picked up her coat and hung it in the front closet then decided to make herself a cup of tea while she edited the work she'd completed that day. As she began to shed her clothes and get ready for bed, it dawned on her that maybe the best gift for Gray would be one of her books, the story of a lonely cat who was befriended by a dancing hamster. She smiled thinking about it. Gray would definitely get a laugh out of this and, no doubt, he'd laugh more recalling how she derived her name.

It was past eleven: too late to be calling her grandparents, but she would call in the morning and ask if she could stay for the weekend. She'd work something out to see Gray, even if just for a few minutes to give him the book as his birthday gift.

A little after one on Saturday, leaving hard food, a can of tuna, and fresh water for Lucy, Samantha left and drove the forty minute journey to Plymouth, arriving just before two in the afternoon. She explained the situation to her grandparents and they loved the idea of Gray receiving the book, especially since it was about a hamster.

Molly laughed, "I remember when your mother told us how she came up with the name for you. I thought it was terrible, but then the more I thought about it, the more I laughed."

Samantha frowned. "Couldn't anyone talk her out of it? I mean, Heather is a nice name, Katie is a good name. Couldn't she bury the name with the hamster?"

Molly laughed again. "Well, think of it this way: it was something she loved, and the name is actually a very nice one. You're not the Katie or Heather type. Samantha suits you. So, how are you going to get the book to John, or should I say to Gray?"

"I've been thinking about that," Samantha said. "Do you think I could call his house? I don't usually do things like that, but I'm not sure of my options with this."

"I don't see any reason why you couldn't call him. Do you have his number?"

"No, but I can look in the phone book." Samantha moved to retrieve the book from under the cupboard where her grandparents' phone sat. She looked up the name Grayson and found only one: Hank Grayson on Hillsborough Street. "Great," Samantha said, "no number for him."

"Call information," Molly suggested. "Maybe his number is unpublished since he's an architect in town."

Samantha tried information and was told that the number was private.

"Call his folks' home." Molly said. "They'll either give you his number or tell him you called. Try that."

Samantha had a serious look on her face; she wasn't sure about making the call, but at her grandmother's urging, she did.

"Mrs. Grayson?" she said to a woman's hello.

"Yes, who's calling please?"

"Mrs. Grayson, my name is Samantha Elwyn. I'm an acquaintance of your son, Gray, John."

"He told us about you," the woman said with a friendly voice. "You're Dan Elwyn's granddaughter. How are you, Dear?"

Samantha smiled, relieved to hear a pleasant voice at the end of the line. "I'm fine, thank you, Mrs. Grayson. Gray told me that Sunday is his birthday and I'm down staying at my grandparents' for the weekend. I was hoping to get in touch with him just to wish him the best."

"Oh," the woman said. "He's out with friends for the day; they went off to some kind of drag-racing event. They're coming back later though, and they plan to have a celebratory evening at Pilgrim's Place here in town. Do you know the place?"

"No," Samantha said. "Is it a restaurant, Mrs. Grayson?"

"Not really. By the way, you don't need to call me Mrs. Grayson; the name is Irene, but I'm called Ree. No, Pilgrim's Place is a sort of, well, a cross between a pub and a dance place. I'm not too fond of it myself, but I suppose when you're young, these places can be entertaining. Anyway, a bunch of them plan to meet there later. You could go there, or you are welcome to come here tomorrow. My daughter is down from New Hampshire with her family and we'll have a family dinner and a cake for Gray."

Samantha hesitated. "Maybe I'll stop in at Pilgrim's Place. I'll see how the day goes. Thank you for the invitation for tomorrow; that's very nice of you."

Ree Grayson was warm and friendly, not at all intimidating as a mother might choose to be with a female calling for her son.

Samantha had not brought much in the way of evening clothing, but she decided that for a pub atmosphere, jeans and a deep red jersey might do. After dinner with her grandparents, she slipped gold sandals onto her feet and fastened gold earrings in place to match a gold heart necklace. With a brushing of her long hair and a touch of red to her lips, she decided that she looked okay. With the book wrapped in plain blue paper, a red length of satin ribbon, and a soft bow, she drove to the pub, arriving there around eight to a lively band and a raucous group of people gyrating on the small dance floor. There were also several people standing around by the bar. The entire atmosphere was not one that Samantha enjoyed; she'd been to many of these places in Boston. Maybe, she thought, it was just too much work meeting someone if this was the scene one had to endure.

As she glanced around, hoping for a glimpse of Gray, several men by the bar watched her with interest. She was a classic beauty, not the type who frequented a place such as this. She went from face to face, looking for the chestnut haired man she knew, but as she decided to get out of there and give up, she saw him on the dance floor, his arms raised high, moving in synchronized motion to the music and a blonde's swirling hips. She watched for a few moments, her lips slightly parted, her heart not wanting her eyes to tell her this truth. Samantha felt for the car keys in her pocket then bolted out of there as fast as she could.

Back early to her grandparents' home, Molly looked up from her crocheting and TV watching as Samantha entered the room. "You're home earlier than I'd expected," she said.

Samantha sat down on the sofa across from her grandmother.

Her grandfather laughed at something he was watching and the two women shook their heads and smiled at his close attention to the humorous show.

"I don't see why he likes this so much," Molly said. "So, did you connect with John Grayson?"

Samantha leaned back against the soft pillows. "No. I should have known better. I should have listened to my gut instinct."

"Why? What do you mean?" Molly asked as she looked at Samantha and stopped working on her shawl.

"Oh," Samantha began as she stood and walked toward a window and then back to her seat, "he's just so, I don't know, unavailable."

"Unavailable? But he went in to Boston and took you out for dinner. That doesn't sound unavailable to me."

"But, Gram, he could take out the princess of wherever. He's got looks, he's got charm. I mean, really, this guy is just too good to be true."

"Now wait a minute," Molly said. "What happened tonight? Did he say something to turn you away?"

"No," Samantha shook her head, "he didn't see me at all. I walked into the place where he'd gone with his friends. I looked around for him, and then I spotted him out on the dance floor with a smiling blonde. No, a *laughing* blonde."

Molly smiled. "So you saw him dancing with another girl? That's what you're upset about? Honey, I can see you being a tad jealous, but gee, the poor guy was just dancing. I wouldn't take that too seriously."

Samantha rubbed her eyes, wishing she could rub away the vision of his tall, well-framed body twisting in time to the music. "I think I'm going to bed, Gram. I'm so tired, and I'll probably head back to Boston fairly early." She walked to each of her grandparents, kissed them both and then went upstairs to her room.

When Samantha opened her eyes that Sunday morning, she lay in bed, realizing that it was Gray's birthday. She had no idea how old he was, but she guessed around thirty. After more than a half hour thinking about everything that had happened, she willed herself to get out of bed, take a shower, then head back to Boston.

Down in her grandparents' warm kitchen, she found her grandfather reading the Boston Globe, its pages spread out all over the kitchen table.

"For goodness sake, Daniel," Molly said, "move that paper so that Sam can sit and have some breakfast."

"It's okay," Samantha said with a smile to her grandfather. "Breakfast isn't for me today. I'll have some coffee to go though. I'm going to head back to Boston. I still have work to do on my book."

"That's not a good idea, Samantha," Molly said. "Breakfast is important. Let me fix you some eggs."

Samantha was about to protest when her grandfather pitched in. "Besides, you're expected at the Grayson house."

"What do you mean?" Samantha said with a quick look to her grandfather.

Without looking up from his paper, Daniel Elwyn said, "I was at McHenry's getting the paper and I ran into Irene Grayson. She said she invited you over for John's birthday. I told her you had a gift for him."

Samantha groaned softly. She would not blame her grandfather for this; it was no one's fault but her own.

Molly looked at her pretty granddaughter and understood her dilemma. "Sweetie, don't fret. If you don't want to be there for the hoopla, just stop in and leave the gift. Since your blabber-mouthed grandfather told them you had a gift, there's not much else you can do."

"But I don't want to run into him," Samantha said, and then she realized that she was whining like a five-year old. "Oh Lord," she said, "I'll drop the darn thing off and then make my getaway."

Molly smiled. "Will you let me make you some breakfast?"

"No, Gram, but thank you. I'll just take my coffee and hit the road. I'll stop at the Grayson's. Thanks for having me," she said as she kissed her grandfather's cheek and her grandmother's forehead, and then she was gone.

She found the Grayson home easily, it's pale gray exterior highlighted with window boxes filled with golden chrysanthemums. She parked her car in the driveway and walked, with the book in her hand, to the front door. She rang the bell and was surprised when a little boy with extraordinary blue eyes opened the door. "Are you Michael?" she asked with a smile.

He wore an expression which questioned how she knew that, and then a woman of about thirty-five came up behind him.

"Hi," Samantha said. "I'm Samantha Elwyn. I was wondering if I could leave this for Gray."

"Oh, hi, Samantha. We were hoping you'd be joining us later. But since you're here, come in."

Samantha stepped inside to the plush carpeted hallway.

"Mother," the woman called toward the kitchen. "Samantha Elwyn is here." And then she turned to Samantha and said, "I'm Suzanne, by the way, Gray's sister. And this is my son, Michael. I'm sorry that my husband and father aren't here to meet you; they went out for a walk."

Samantha smiled and nodded at the same time that Irene Grayson came down the hall, drying her hands on a green checkered dishtowel.

"Well, Gray wasn't kidding when he told us you had hair just like his. Samantha, it's nice to meet you, Dear." The woman extended her hand to Samantha and they touched briefly. At that point, the book, wrapped in its blue paper was handed to Irene.

"Would you mind giving this to Gray for me? It's just kind of a little joke; he'll understand."

"Won't you be joining us later?" Irene asked.

"No. I really can't. But thank you so much for asking me. I appreciate it."

"All right," the attractive woman said, "but I'm sure Gray will be sorry to have missed you."

Samantha looked down for a moment then back up into the eyes of Suzanne and then her mother. "I should be going," she said. "It was nice to meet you."

Behind the steering wheel in her car, Samantha couldn't start the engine and put it into reverse fast enough. She wanted to get out of there, back to the safety of her own apartment in Boston.

She was working on her book and eating a bowl of Cheerios when the phone rang at around five-thirty.

"Hi," he said.

Samantha swallowed the last bit of cereal then placed the bowl on the floor next to her computer. "Hi," she said. She instinctively wanted to wish him a happy birthday, but she held back.

"Thank you for the book," he said. "I laughed when 1 saw that it was about a hamster and, of course, I had to explain it a bit to my family."

"Of course," Samantha said dryly.

There was a noted silence. "Are you okay?" he asked. "You don't sound very chipper today."

"I'm fine," she said.

"Okay. Well, I wish you'd have stuck around to have dinner and cake with us, but I suppose this is a busy time of year for you at the museum. I tried to call you Friday night. I was hoping to see you this weekend."

Samantha shifted the phone to her other ear and walked away from the computer to the window with the view. She said nothing in response.

"Hey," he said, "is everything really okay with you? You're awfully quiet."

"Does that imply that I'm usually awfully noisy?"

Gray said nothing at first, and then he began, "What are you doing later?"

"Working," she said.

"Working. Well that's a ridiculous thing to do on my birthday. I know you were down here and went back to Boston this morning, so I'll come in there."

"Why would you do that? Your sister is there with her family; your mother prepared a nice dinner. Why would you travel into Boston on your birthday?"

"To complete my day," he said softly.

Samantha swallowed and closed her eyes for just a moment. Again, she said nothing.

"Samantha? Did you hear me? My family celebrated at two, so I'm not abandoning them."

"Yes," she said, "I heard you, but I'm not sure I get the point."

"Really? I thought we connected very well during our evening in the North End. What's going on, Sam? What am I missing?"

Samantha sat down on a nearby chair, her eyes on the patterned rug. "I went to the pub where you were Saturday night."

"You did? For Pete's sake, how come I didn't know you were there? Did you see me?"

She smiled. "Oh, yes. You were having a good time out on the dance floor."

Gray was quiet. He understood what she meant. "I think I get it," he said. "You saw me dancing with a pretty blonde, right?"

"That would be accurate."

"Okay," he said, "but what isn't accurate is that all the guys know her which is why she can be fun to dance with, but nothing else. I'm not saying she's a bad person, but her reputation for being a little light in the brain department is well known. She's harmless, Sam. I danced with her at her invitation. If you'd been there, or if I'd had any idea you were going to be there, I would have been waiting for you, not out dancing with Karry. When I called Friday night, I should have invited you to the gathering at the pub and at my parents' home. I was going to if I'd talked to you, but I'm not too good at leaving messages on a mechanical device. I'm sorry about that. I guess I hoped you'd be there when I called and, when you weren't, I just put the phone down. It's my only fault," he said softly.

Samantha smiled. "I'm sure."

"How about if I leave here and arrive at your place in an hour? We could go out for a late supper."

"Not tonight," she said.

"Okay, you can bring the cat."

Samantha almost laughed; he was trying very hard to lighten their conversation.

"Sam, I'd like to see you."

She looked at the clock over her mantle. "It's nearly six, Gray;

you wouldn't be here for another hour, then dinner? Isn't it kind of late to do that when we both have to work tomorrow?"

"It's my birthday," he said.

She hesitated. "Do you like pizza?"

"Love it," he said.

"How about if I order a pizza to be delivered in about an hour? That way we don't have to go out."

Gray smiled into the phone. "Maybe I'll get to meet your cat, Lucy. She's going to love me."

"I see."

"Okay, then, pizza in an hour with Sam and Lucy. What more could a guy ask for on his thirty-first birthday?"

Samantha smiled and hung up the phone when the conversation concluded. She finished with her work, shut the computer down, fed Lucy, ordered the pizza, then changed from her jeans and tan jersey to a better pair of jeans and a soft gray shirt. Twenty-five minutes later, Gray arrived carrying the pizza.

"I met the delivery guy in the elevator," he explained.

"I'll get the money for you," she said as she reached for her purse.

"No, forget it," Gray said.

"It's your birthday," she said and insisted that he take the cash.

Gray looked at the money she'd placed in his hand and shook his head. "Well, since I can't convince you to let me pay, thank you."

"You're welcome," she said. "Would you like a glass of wine or a beer to go with the pizza?"

"A beer would be perfect," he said, "and then maybe some coffee. Do you have coffee?"

"I do. I'll make some after we eat." She passed him a cold bottle of beer and a tall glass, then retrieved plates and napkins. "We can sit at the coffee table if you'd like."

"Sounds good," he said as the cat made her entrance and walked right over to him. "Hey, it's Lucy, and I think she approves of me."

Samantha sat down and took a bite of her pizza. She didn't want to insult him by telling him that Lucy liked to lick the cheese from pizza and, if given the chance, she might also sip at his beer.

"I'm glad you agreed to see me tonight," he said as he wiped tomato sauce from his mouth. "I needed this."

Samantha was amazed at how in sync they were, their conversation not at all forced, everything was genuine. But still, her mind told her to back off, to be aware that this was a man who could prove to be a problem in his offerings of good looks and charm. It was exhilarating and it was frightening. She was going to move slowly with the development of this relationship, or maybe not at all.

Gray looked at her, loving the way her hair cascaded down her back and over her shoulders. "Is everything really okay? I get the feeling it isn't. What's up, Sam?"

"Nothing," she said. "I'm a little tired I think. I'm very glad that my work at the museum is kind of taking care of itself until after the holidays. I have a deadline for this new book I'm writing, so, feeling a bit of pressure."

Gray looked at her and sat back with the last of his beer.

"I promised coffee," she said. "I'll go start it. I'll just be a minute."

"I'd like that," he said as he watched her move to the small kitchen. "Thank you."

When she returned to the living room he said, "I didn't tell you: I read the book you gave me to Michael and he loved it. I expect they're available in the book stores? I'd like to get him the entire set for Christmas."

Samantha had seated herself back in the corner of the sofa and then she stood.

"They're in the bookstores, but I have several copies of them all. I found them a couple of days ago when searching for one requested by a friend. I can give you a set; there are eight of them so far. I'm working on the ninth. I'll get them for you."

Before he could protest, she was gone and then back with a shopping bag filled with the colorfully covered books.

Gray looked inside and lifted one out. "These are great. Thank you so much. What do I owe you?"

Samantha wanted to say, your life, but she said that they were part of the publishing deal and hadn't cost her a dime. He was welcome to them.

"He'll love these. Maybe I'll pick him up a stuffed animal like one of your characters to go with the books. I promise, it won't be a hamster."

Samantha smiled. "Yeah, I think I'm going to regret the day I told you about that."

Gray laughed as Samantha walked to the kitchen for the coffee, asking him if he took either cream, sugar, or both. "Black," he said, "I'm easy."

A short time later at the elevator, the bag of books in one hand, he leaned forward and kissed her: long, deep, familiar. It all felt so right.

"Thank you for tonight," he said. "I'll call you."

Fifteen minutes later the phone rang. "Hi," he said.

Samantha smiled. "Hi. This phone stuff is getting to be a habit," she teased.

"A bad habit or a good habit?"

She smiled and was glad he couldn't see her. "I'm not so sure," she said.

"Ah, a non-committing woman. Now, you wouldn't want me to be lonely all the way home would you? I just got on the expressway. There's no traffic; it's great."

"Good," she said.

"Did I tell you I loved tonight? And by the way, you have a very well-mannered cat. Once when you got up to get something in the kitchen, she attempted to eat your pizza. I told her no and she backed off."

Samantha looked at Lucy who was sitting next to her on the sofa. She whispered *traitor* to her and hoped he didn't hear. "Yes, well she does like pizza."

"You might have warned me," Gray said. "All I need is to develop fur-ball or some other infectious disease from the cat. Thanks."

Samantha laughed. "As long as you don't bathe her with your tongue, I think you're safe on the fur-ball issue."

"Great. I might just toss my pizza right here on the highway."

Samantha laughed again and reached out to pat Lucy.

They talked for another fifteen minutes until he found himself in the Hanover area. At that point he told her he was going to stop to fill his gas tank and they said goodnight.

Samantha sat for a few minutes thinking about being with him. It was exciting, yet so much like being with an old friend.

Deciding that it was all out of her control, she ran water for a soak in the tub and then returned to the computer to work more on her book. It had been a simple decision, but not one to easily implement.

He was saturating her with his being. She felt fulfilled when she was with him and lonely when he was gone. This wasn't good. This was becoming dangerous and the water for her bath was growing cool. She shed her clothes and stepped in, adding more hot water and a few squirts of lavender soap. She leaned back and closed her eyes; Lucy sat nearby on a little chair.

When the phone rang, she opened her eyes and grunted, angry with herself for not bringing the portable into the bathroom where she could reach it. Was it Gray again she wondered?

When the ringing ceased, she pulled the plug in the old claw-foot tub and climbed out of the tepid water, a large towel draped around her body. Nearly dry, the phone rang again. This time she hurried to answer it and noticed that no message had been left from the time before.

"Hello?"

"Sam, I was afraid you were away or something. It's Will. How are you, Sweetie?"

Sam closed her eyes for a moment and smiled. "I'm fine, Will. How about you?"

"I'm excellent. I'm going to be in Boston for a week and I want to see you. No, let me rephrase that, I *have* to see you. No excuses. I don't care how busy you are or that you're probably working on your one hundredth book. You need to put some time aside so that we can be together."

Samantha smiled again. "I hear you. Don't worry. I'll carve out some time for you, Will. Haven't I always?"

"I knew you would." he said. "Listen, any chance we could get down to Plymouth so I can see your grandparents? I'd love to visit with them too."

"Sure," Samantha said. "They'd be very sad if they didn't get the opportunity to see you. How's everything in Chicago?"

"It couldn't be better, unless you were here, of course."

"Oh, of course," Samantha said as she dried her ankles and sat down on the sofa. "I miss you, Will. I'm so glad you'll be in town for a few days. I need some 'Will' time, just like when we were in college. Late night coffees in Harvard Square, calzones from Michelangelo's. We've had some serious fun."

"Incredible fun," he said. "I'll call you when I arrive, but set aside the coming week for me. We'll Christmas shop."

Samantha smiled. "You've got it."

When the call ended and she leaned back against the sofa pillows, clutching her large white towel, she felt the gladness of talking with Will, of knowing he was coming into town soon, begin to fade. The stronger image was one of Gray. He'd found a way to crawl under her skin to make her thoughts return to him, to make her want him. She stood up and walked to her bedroom where she pulled a knee-length nightgown over her head, dropping the towel, and then she crept beneath the bed's covers. She wished she hadn't met Gray, yet she felt enriched and filled with something powerful because she had.

She didn't know what to do about her tumultuous feelings. What, she wondered, does one do with a derisive heart?

Chapter Four

On Monday evening, as Samantha put the final editing of her book to the test, reading it aloud to herself, the telephone rang. She thought it might be Will, but instead she heard the deep, melodic voice of Gray.

"Hey," he said, "just wanted to touch base with you and thank you for last night. The pizza party was the best."

Samantha smiled and sat down on one arm of her sofa. "Good," she said, "I aim to please."

"And you do," he said. "So, when do I see you again? Are you free anytime this coming weekend?"

"Actually, no," she said as she slid down into the cushions of the sofa. "An old college friend is coming into town and I expect to be out and about, Christmas shopping and such."

"Ah," Gray said, "two women loose in the malls. That could get scary."

Samantha lightly bit her bottom lip. "It's not a woman," she said, and wondered why she'd felt it necessary to mention that. Was she trying to push Gray away? Was he too much for her to handle?

"Oh. I guess that'll teach me to assume the obvious."

Samantha was stuck for words. On one hand she wanted to draw him to her and, on the other, she wanted him to keep his irresistible distance. She hated that her insecure thoughts were pushing them apart.

"Are you still there?" he asked when she'd said nothing.

"Yes, I'm here."

"Is there anything you'd like to tell me? Am I interested in a girl who's already been spoken for?"

Samantha closed her eyes and let her head rest against the back of the chenille sofa. "It's a friendship," she said. "Will and I have been close for a long time."

"I see."

Samantha opened her eyes and sat up straight. She wanted to tell him that he didn't see at all, that Will was not the man of her dreams, and that she wanted too much to be wherever Gray was. It frightened her how much she cared.

"He'll only be around for a week," she said softly.

Gray was silent for a few moments. "So, should I call you in a week?"

Samantha thought his voice sounded defensive. She understood that she was hurting him, the way it would hurt her if he was entertaining a former college friend who happened to be female. "Sure," she said, and knew that it was too little to say.

On Wednesday, Will arrived in town and on Thursday they drove to Plymouth to see Molly and Dan Elwyn. Molly prepared Will's favorite meal, chicken with dumplings and apple pie for dessert.

"You have no idea how I've been dreaming of this meal," Will said to Molly as he gave her a hug. "In Chicago I eat out all the time, mostly at one particular restaurant where they feature Italian cuisine. It's good, really great, but one does get tired of eating mostly Italian."

Molly laughed. "Well, I'm glad you weren't here last night for supper; we had spaghetti and meatballs."

Will made a face. "While I'm sure it was divine, I'm glad I wasn't here too. But these dumplings, these are a fantastic treat."

"How are your mother and your grandparents?" Dan Elwyn asked after swallowing a forkful of apple pie.

"Everyone's fine," Will said. "They all knew I was coming here, of course, and asked me to say hello to each one of you."

"Your grandmother has been one of my dearest friends for fifty years," Molly said. "I don't see her often enough."

"No one does," Will said with a laugh. "She's the busiest woman I know, always involved in something. I hope I have that kind of energy in another forty years."

Molly looked at her husband and he winked at her. These young ones thought that being in your seventies was having one foot in the grave.

"Sam," her grandfather said, "you should take Will out for a drink later. There's a new place open in town, right on the main street. They have a guitarist and people are saying it's enjoyable."

"That sounds nice," Will said as he looked at Samantha.

"Okay," she said, "we'll give it a shot." She was eating and thinking that she had hoped to be invisible while in Plymouth with Will. But what were the chances, she wondered, that she would run into anyone in the middle of the week. Will was very handsome. She didn't want to worry Gray, or did she? Maybe he deserved it after dancing with the slinky blonde. "What's the name of the place, Grampa?"

"Let me think," he said. "It's something like The Salty Dog Cafe. I think that's it, yes, The Salty Dog. Looks nice at night when we've driven past. Nice lighting makes all the difference."

"Absolutely," Will said, "it sounds great to me. How about you, Sam, are you up for it?"

She smiled. "Sure, why not?"

When they'd finished their meal and Samantha helped to clear the table, Will helped her into the long, forest green coat she'd worn down from Boston. "Are you really okay with this? You seemed a bit hesitant."

"No," Samantha said as she smiled at her friend. "I'm not at all hesitant. But we can't be there too long; you have that meeting in the morning, don't you? It's a good forty-five minutes back into Boston from here."

"You're right, but we'll give ourselves an hour or so and then we can head back into town." He walked toward the kitchen where he hugged and thanked Molly for a wonderful evening, and then he made his way into the parlor where he said goodnight with a handshake to Dan. Samantha said goodnight with kisses to them both, telling them she'd see them again soon.

When they walked into The Salty Dog Cafe, Will smiled and looked at Samantha. "This place is hot," he said. "I like this very much."

They made their way to a small bistro table and ordered a glass of wine each with coffee to follow. The guitarist was immersed in his tune. Everyone gave their attention to the music and a few couples moved slowly on the ten-foot square of dance floor. Samantha looked at the swaying figures, glad not to see Gray out there embraced by some adoring female.

When the guitarist's rhythm drifted into a soft Spanish beat, Will grabbed Samantha by the wrist and pulled her to her feet.

"What are we doing?" she asked as she left her drink on the table and reluctantly followed him out onto the dance floor.

"The Maluka," he said with a mischievous smile.

"The what?"

"Come on, we're making this up as we go, just move to the music, Baby."

Samantha laughed as she tried to follow Will, her flowing chestnut hair moving like wind-driven feathers against her back and shoulders of the ankle length black dress. By the time the piece was over, they were the only pair on the dance floor and finished with a worthy applause from the other seated patrons.

As they started back to their table, Will tried to detain her for another dance, but she pulled him toward their seats. "No, enough already. I'm thirsty."

As they sat down, Samantha was aware that someone was walking toward her. She looked up to see Gray standing at her side.

Neither of them spoke at first and Will looked puzzled.

"Hi," Samantha finally said to ease the tension.

Will looked at Samantha and then at Gray. He stood, reached out a hand to shake and introduced himself. "Hello, I'm Will Parks."

"John Grayson," he said, not taking his eyes off Samantha. "Nice to see you, Sam."

She looked uncomfortable, but in one way she thought it was poetic justice that he would see her dancing with Will.

"Will is my friend from college," she said. "We had dinner with my grandparents tonight and, in a short while, we're heading back into Boston. Will has an early morning appointment."

Gray did not comment. Will moved his chair a bit toward Samantha and invited Gray to pull another chair up to join them. "Sit down," he said. "Let's hear how you two know one another."

"I can tell Samantha filled you in on me," Gray said with a glance to her.

Samantha felt her cheeks flush as she sipped the last of her wine.

"Not really," Will said with a quick look to each of them. "Sammy, I'm going to get our coffees. Can I get one for you, John?"

"No. I'm set, thanks," Gray said and then turned his attention to Samantha as Will walked over to the counter bar area. "So," Gray said to Samantha, "are we even now?"

She looked at him with a very serious expression. "I wasn't trying to even things up, Gray. I had no idea you'd be here tonight. In fact, isn't your hang out more The Pilgrim's Place?"

Gray smiled. "I don't think I have a hang out. A friend of mine is tonight's guitarist. He invited me to come by. They feature several different musicians here; it tends to be pot luck."

Samantha felt very ashamed to have been so vindictive and to have sounded so much of a witch.

Will came back with the coffees in paper containers and it was then that Samantha suggested they take the brew on the road and head back to the city.

"It was nice to meet you, John," Will said. "I hope we'll see you again sometime."

Gray shook hands with Will, but he had no words for either of them as they turned and left the cafe.

On their way back to Samantha's car, Will asked about John Grayson. "Okay, so who the heck is he? He's one good-looking man. You didn't mention him to me, Sam, and that usually means you're interested but you don't want to talk about it."

Samantha unlocked her car and they got in out of the December cold. She started the engine then sipped the hot coffee before putting the car into reverse and then into drive. "He's someone I met on the docks at Thanksgiving," she said.

"He's more than that," Will said. "Come on, fess up."

Samantha smiled in the dark of the car and pulled out in the direction of the highway. "He's, I don't know, he's Gray."

"He doesn't look gray to me," Will teased.

Samantha smiled. "He goes by that name, Gray."

"And you're interested in him."

"Unfortunately," she said.

"Why? What's going on with him?"

"You saw him, he's gorgeous. He's smart, he's charming, and he's trouble."

Will laughed. "Oh-oh, someone's falling hard."

"I am not," Samantha said. "I refuse."

"Oh, right. It happens just like that," Will said. "Like we can choose who we fall in love with."

"Well, I know what you're saying," she said, "but there comes a time when you have to ask yourself what you're going to do about it. I mean, this guy is pure problem. I don't have to follow my disastrous emotions. I have a brain."

"Sam, Sweetie, you're kidding yourself. This man obviously cares about you. By the way, I never saw anyone with your hair color until tonight. Did you realize his and yours are exactly the same? Whew, guess your kids would have beautiful hair."

"Stop!" Samantha said and laughed. "Hair color is not a reason to spend your life with someone."

"I've known of worse reasons," he said. "Besides, there's a neon sign where your heart is, and the same goes for him. You two are an amazing match."

"Let's get off this subject," Samantha said as she drove the arrow-straight road back to Boston. "Are we Christmas shopping after your meeting tomorrow?"

"Absolutely. I have a list and I want to hit the Galleria. I have it in mind to buy everything I need - simple yet wonderful gifts. Mother loves the purses at that fancy little shop with the green awnings. I want one of those handbags for her. I'm a very efficient shopper, as you know."

"I do know," Samantha said. "I learned to be a good shopper from you and I think of you every time I need a gift. Zeroing in on what the person truly likes is so much more rewarding than picking up something generic and calling it a gift. I hate it when people give me a candle, or a crystal vase."

"Shall I phone your hunky boyfriend and warn him?" Will teased.

Samantha reached over and nudged Will on his left forearm.

Will laughed. "You're tough," he said to her. "You're right up there on the love scale with my mother and grandmother, but man alive, you're a hard sell."

"Why do you say that?" Samantha asked.

"Because it's the truth, Sweetie. You're a wonderful person, but you're as fussy as fussy gets. I can't imagine you not jumping at the chance with this Gray guy."

Samantha made a face in the dark of her car, keeping her hands gripped on the wheel and her eyes on the road. "He's undoubtedly interesting, Will, but think how hard it would be to keep someone like him on a leash."

Will threw his head back and laughed. "Only you could equate this man with a dog. Why would you want to keep him on a leash? The way he looks at you, Sam, I think he'd be more worried about how to keep you. Have you looked in the mirror lately? Have you noticed the charming books you write? Have you taken note how dear you are to your family and friends? Come on, any guy is going to be watchful of his own actions so as not to lose you. Your Gray is incredible, but so are you."

Samantha drove carefully, approaching their turn off in Boston. She was quiet, thinking, wondering. She was disappointed in herself for not following through with what she really wanted, out of pure fear.

"So," he continued, "are we on for the Galleria tomorrow? I have a brief seminar in the morning. I should be through by noon. We can go for lunch, then shop. What do you think?"

Samantha pulled up in front of the hotel where Will was staying. "I think it sounds great. Call me when you're through and we'll take off. Maybe you can help me to decide what to get for Mom and Dad. It's so hard where they're on a vessel much of the time. They have the condo, but they're hardly ever there. They don't need anything for the house; in fact, they got rid of tons of stuff when they moved into this smaller space. As for clothes, even that is an issue because they wear these really ugly jumpsuits on the ship. I wrack my brain trying to think what to get them."

"We'll think about it," Will said. "I can see where it could be a challenge to find them the right gifts." He leaned over to her and gave her a kiss, then climbed out of the car and disappeared into the building.

Samantha pulled away and drove to her apartment. Being with Will made her feel alive and not so alone. Having parents out to sea, brothers in California, friends all over the world creating and working at their careers, she felt that the stable part of her life was definitely in Plymouth with her grandparents. It was the place she could call home.

Inside her apartment, Samantha was greeted by Lucy who rubbed her soft fur against Sam's ankles and purred loudly, her declaration that she was glad to have her home. "Hi. Lucy," she said as she reached down to pet the cat. "Come on, I have some chicken in the frig for you; I'll heat it for just a few seconds in the microwave, and then you can dine royally. How's that?"

The cat purred louder and followed Samantha to the kitchen.

As she entered the living room, leaving Lucy to eat her dinner, Samantha noticed that the little red light on her answering machine was blinking. Gray? She looked at the number on the caller ID. It was her grandmother. Sam pressed a button and listened.

"Hi, Dear. I suppose you're still out with Will, but I forgot to tell you that John Grayson came by a couple of days ago. He left a lovely bouquet of mums for us, but he also extended an invitation to us and to you. His parents are hosting a Christmas fundraiser to benefit the local food pantry. It will be at their home, an open house sort of thing where you can stay for ten minutes or hours, and everyone brings food items. It's this coming Sunday from three to seven. If Will is going to be around, I'm sure he'd be welcome. Let me know, Dear. You know we'd love to see you."

Samantha held the phone in her hands for a few moments, then she placed it back on its receiver and sat down. Sunday with Gray. She wanted that. Will was leaving on Saturday morning, so there were no complications there. It was after eleven now, so she would call her grandparents tomorrow to tell them she would join them at the Grayson home.

The next day Will phoned Samantha around ten-thirty to tell her that the work day was done and he'd love to meet her at the Galleria for their lunch and shopping spree.

Seated in a designated restaurant space at a small table, Will saw her coming toward him wearing a long black skirt and a short red jacket, her beautiful hair swirling about as she walked.

"Hello, Beautiful," he said as he stood and reached out to her with a hug.

Samantha smiled. "You're good for my ego," she said.

"Well," he said, "anyone would have to be blind not to see that you're beautiful, but, yes, I'm a good ego booster."

Samantha smiled. "Modest too."

Will laughed. "So, what are we having for lunch? The last time we were here I had that walnut salad, you know, the one with chicken, cranberries and stuff. It was really good."

Samantha smiled. "I think you should have it again; you liked it a lot. I think I'll have the house salad. They have greens I've never seen anywhere else and I love them. Besides, if I have salad for lunch, I can have a hot fudge sundae later."

Will laughed. "Okay then, we're decided," he said to the waiter. Then to Samantha he said, "Do you have a place you want to start? I have a list, what about you?"

Samantha took a sip of her water. "This is more about your

shopping needs. I live here, I can come anytime, but yes, I have things I may pick up as we go along. I already have my brothers' gifts, I bought them each binoculars. It's funny, they were tough little creatures as kids, but they've softened. They live near a place where there are many wild parrots and they love watching them. I thought the binoculars would be a good idea for each of them."

"What a terrific idea," Will said. "I have a friend who lives in a condo overlooking Chicago's shore line. Binoculars would make a super gift for him. What else have you bought so far?"

"I bought a fleece jacket for Grandpa and a really pretty hair clip for my grandmother. Her hair is so beautiful; I love those shades of silver and white, and she wears hair jewelry every day. I'm just stumped on my parents. But I have your gift," she teased.

"What is it?" he asked, as he was about to take a mouthful of his food.

"I'm not telling. You'll have to take it home with you and wait until Christmas."

"Oh, yeah, that's going to happen! I'll have the paper ripped off the gift as soon as you're out of sight."

Samantha laughed. "Yes. I know." She had purchased him a Red Sox shirt and baseball cap to match. He was a big fan, even though he lived in Chicago and loved the Cubs.

"That's okay," he said, "I found something for you in Chicago and I think you'll like it. It's not a candle, nothing generic, I promise."

Samantha smiled. "Are we ready to do some damage to our bank accounts? I'm dying to get out and look. I'm hoping to jar my senses into finding gifts for Mom and Dad."

That evening Will and Samantha dined together for their Christmas celebration; he would be leaving for Chicago the next day. With a candle flickering at the table and soft Christmas carols in the background, Samantha couldn't help but allow her thoughts to stray toward Gray and she wondered what he was doing at this very moment in time.

"Where are you?" Will asked after he'd sipped his wine and studied her serene face.

Samantha smiled. "Right here, with you."

"Oh, no you're not. You're not fooling me, Samantha Elwyn; I know that look."

"So," she said, "are you pleased with today's purchases? I think you've picked up some wonderful gifts."

"I think so too," he said and decided not to press her on where her mind was. He pretty much figured it was in Plymouth with a chestnut haired man named Gray.

"And tomorrow you leave. I'll miss you. I wish we didn't live so far away from one another. I love these get-togethers and would enjoy them more often, like once a month, at least."

"My pockets aren't that deep, Sammy. I love seeing you too, but you bring out the shopper in me. You should come to Chicago again sometime. When you were there last, we had a good time out at those blues clubs."

"We did," Samantha said with a nod of her head. "It was fun."

The next day Will returned to Chicago, leaving Samantha feeling a little lost. She hadn't heard a word from Gray except through her grandmother regarding the invitation for the food pantry event. As she sat on her sofa with a new magazine and Lucy at her side, the phone beckoned to her. She answered hopefully, "Hello?"

"Hi. Sweetheart, how good it is to hear your voice."

"Hi, Gram. How's everything going?"

"Fine, Dear. Will still around or did he go home?"

"He left. We had a nice time. We shopped, went to the Pops one evening, and, of course, tried lots of restaurants. You know Will."

Molly Elwyn smiled. "Oh, yes, that boy likes to eat. Well, now that he's gone and your museum schedule is lessened, how about coming here to stay with us? It's only ten days 'til Christmas. I can't believe it, but it's coming whether I'm ready or not."

Samantha put her magazine aside and pulled Lucy onto her lap. "I know," she said, "the holidays sneak up on us, don't they? As for me joining you in Plymouth, I'd have to bring my little pal with me again."

"Well, you know that's fine with us. You can keep her in your room so that she doesn't escape and go roaming the streets of Plymouth, but Lucy is a most welcome guest. Pack her suitcase and bring her along. There's no sense you being in Boston by yourself. Come and stay with us. We've got that gathering at the Grayson's too. You'll go, won't you?

"Yes, I'll go. It sounds like a worthy cause and a nice time. Is your tree up?" Samantha asked. "I have a tiny one in my kitchen, but that's it."

"Ours is up. You know what your grandfather is like. He loves the tree. We put it up two nights ago and I will admit it looks very cheerful. Every night we have a warm cider before bed and a nice half hour or so by the tree."

"It sounds very inviting. I think I'll pop over to the museum just to make sure they're all set, then I'll grab Lucy and a few pieces of clothing. I'll be down, probably sometime this afternoon. I'll stop for some pastries; Grampa likes those rum slices."

Molly laughed. "Yes, he wears them well. Anytime you arrive is fine with us. I'm so glad you're coming, Honey. This time of year feels lonely if no one's around; it seems like the house should be bustling with memory making activities."

"Okay, then. I'm excited for the coming days, and Mom and Dad should be here in a week or so. We'll rock that old town and have a wonderful Christmas.'

Molly smiled and wiped away a stray tear. "We will," she agreed.

Later, with Lucy in her carrier in the seat next to Samantha, they made their way out of Boston and onto the highway south. Samantha sang Christmas carols to Lucy who blinked and seemed unimpressed. Forty-five minutes later, Samantha pulled into her grandparents' driveway, put the car in park and turned off the engine. She stepped out of the car and, with the pet carrier in one hand and the box of pastries in the other, she met her grandfather's smile as he opened the front door to her.

"Hello, my little one," he said as he reached for the pet carrier, saying meow and then hello to Lucy. He placed it down at his feet then reached for Samantha and a hug.

"It's so good to have you here," he said, "both of you. Merry Christmas! Shall I take Lucy upstairs or do you want her to have a look around in the house?"

"I'll run her upstairs to my room. I'm sure she's frazzled with the ride; she doesn't think much of the car. I still have the litter box down cellar, right? I could get her settled in."

"You take her on up; I'll get the litter box. How about food and water?"

"I have her dishes and food in the car. I'll get them in a

minute and then she can settle down. I brought her favorite blanket too; she can cuddle up with that."

Dan Elwyn smiled. "Well, she'll be fine. It's not like she hasn't been here before, and she's always been a perfect guest."

They each went their separate ways, making Lucy safe and comfortable, then they met in the kitchen where Molly assembled the ingredients for making fudge.

"Hi, Gram," Samantha said as she kissed her grandmother's soft cheek. "It smells so chocolaty in here, it's wonderful."

Molly smiled and looked at her pretty granddaughter. "I love making fudge: it's necessary to sample a bit here and there, and it does make the kitchen smell good, doesn't it?"

"It does," Samantha said as she poured herself a cup of hot coffee. "It looks like you're making a ton of it."

"Well, I am. Actually, I make about thirty pounds in all. The church gets twenty pounds to sell at their bazaar and the other ten pounds goes to family and friends. Your father will expect me to have saved him a pound too. Every year, even when they've been out to sea, I've sent the fudge."

"Anything I can do to help?" Samantha asked.

"Sure," Molly said. "After we have a bite of lunch, you can help me with all the measuring. I make it in five pound batches, it just comes out better that way, don't ask me why. I love making it, but by the time I've made six batches, believe me, I don't want to see fudge again until at least Easter."

Samantha laughed. "Okay, so what will we have for lunch? I brought the pastries from the North End. Would you like me to run out for some subs or a salad?"

"No," Molly said. "What would you think of grilled cheese on a nice dark rye?"

"Perfect," Samantha said as she moved out of her grandmother's way and sat down at the table with her coffee.

"So, now that Will's gone back to Chicago, what have you been doing for fun?"

"He's only been gone for a few hours, but this week I managed to finish my book and deliver it to the publisher. I've cleaned my apartment and sorted out some clothes for the shelters, and mostly, I guess, I've just been bumming around with Lucy."

Molly washed her hands and looked at Samantha with a serious expression. "Gee, that sounds like fun."

Samantha laughed and so did Molly.

"Have you been hearing from John Grayson?"

Samantha put her cup down on the table. "Not really, except through you about tomorrow."

Molly dried her hands and reached for the frying pan overhead. "Really? Why not? I thought you two were very nice together."

Samantha swallowed and smiled for her grandmother. "I like him; he's a terrific guy."

"I hear a *but* in that reply," Molly said.

"Okay," Samantha began, "the *but* you heard is a bit of concern. He's almost *too* terrific. I mean, Gram, you know him; he's just about everything any woman would be looking for. I don't want to be one of his many admirers."

"Well, he can't help who admires him. What he can help is for whom he yearns."

Samantha smiled. "Now yearn is a word you don't hear every day. And I doubt that he's yearning for anyone in particular. I'd bet he enjoys all the attention he gets."

Molly stopped and looked at Samantha, the cheese for the sandwiches in her hands. "Well, if that's so, I wonder why he's stopped in here a couple of times this past week. I don't think he's that caught up with his old high school teacher. And when he called the other night about going to his folks' for the party, he asked if we knew where you were. Apparently he'd been trying to call your apartment. -

"Really? Well, if he called, he didn't leave a message." And then she remembered that he said he didn't like talking to a mechanical device and rarely leaves messages.

"Maybe you should let him know you're in Plymouth now until after Christmas."

Samantha sipped her warm coffee and watched her grandmother slice cheese for the sandwiches. "Maybe," she said.

Molly turned around to the stove turning the heat on beneath the frying pan.

Samantha placed her cup down and thought about Gray. She was looking forward to seeing him tomorrow, so much that her heart felt in competition with her mind. It was Christmas, she decided, and she was taking this chance as a gift to herself.

Chapter Five

Sunday morning when Samantha opened her eyes she smiled; Lucy was sitting on her pillow, her front paws on Samantha's flowing hair. "Hey, you," she said as she stroked the cat's paws with one finger, "are you my alarm clock today?"

The cat purred and sat up straight as if to say that it was time for something other than sleeping.

Samantha lifted the thick quilt and other covers then moved her legs out of the comfortable old bed, her feet into slippers. The sun was neon bright and the sky held only the purest color of blue. She squinted against the light but loved it. This was the beginning of a beautiful day.

While she dressed in jeans and a warm brown sweater, she thought about what she would pick up to donate at the Grayson's food pantry event. Samantha smiled at the thought of seeing Gray. It was going to be the beginning of her new and brave attitude, *do not fear falling.* And she loved the idea of a holiday gathering that sought to do more than have a good time.

In her grandparents' kitchen eating scrambled eggs and toast, Samantha asked what they would be taking for cans or boxes of food.

"We have a good supply of tuna fish and cranberry sauce," Molly said, "but I thought we'd stop at the store and pick up a few seasonal items as well. Pumpkin pie mix and crusts, tins of vegetables, things like that."

"I suppose everything non-perishable is good," Samantha said. "I was thinking of cake mixes, puddings, maybe pasta sauce and pasta."

"And baked beans," Daniel Elwyn added. "They're always a source of good, healthy food."

Molly turned and winked at Samantha. "He loves beans, that's why he thought of them. But he's right, they're healthy. I have a nice big laundry basket I can part with; we'll take it along and fill it up. And I'll take a pound of my fudge to the Grayson's."

Samantha smiled and nodded. "That's a nice idea. Maybe 1 should bring them something too."

"I don't think you have to, Sweetheart. This is more about bringing the pantry items. Besides, you helped with the fudge; we'll say it's from all of us Elwyn's."

When breakfast was over, Samantha asked if there was something she could do to be of help. Molly had dinner all planned, everything was in order and she was going to work on a scarf she was knitting for a friend. Samantha decided to write a few Christmas cards while spending some time with Lucy, who contentedly slept in Samantha's lap.

The party at Grayson's was beginning at three. At two, Samantha chose what she would wear, a knee-length dark gray skirt with a cream-colored silk shirt.

"You look beautiful," Daniel Elwyn said to his granddaughter as she approached the living room where he sat.

"Thank you," she said as she kissed his forehead. "Is Gram upstairs or in the kitchen?"

"I think she's still upstairs getting ready. It's so nice to have you here with us. It feels like Christmas already."

"I love being here," Samantha said. "Plymouth and your home have always represented stability to me. I feel safe here."

"You should move here," Molly said as she came from behind Samantha.

"One day I will," Samantha said with a smile. "Boston has been wonderful for me, everything pertaining to my work is there, but it doesn't feel like home. Someday I'll buy a house down here, where I can be near to the sea and the people I love."

Molly hugged her granddaughter. "Are we ready to shop and then go by the Grayson's for a while?"

"I'm ready," Samantha said as she gave a hand to her grandfather, urging him out of his comfortable chair.

In a neighborhood grocery store the three of them selected several items to donate to the food pantry. Samantha picked up two pounds of coffee and asked if that might be appropriate.

"Oh, yes, good thought," Molly said. "And tea, we should get a few boxes of tea, and maybe hot cocoa."

Samantha smiled watching her enthusiastic grandparents

scurry about the store, filling the cart to its brim. They checked out and then headed for the Grayson's home which was decorated in tiny white lights and candles at the windows.

Just as they were about to knock on the front door it opened and Gray's sister, Suzanne, stood there, a smile on her face welcoming them in from the cold.

"I'm so glad you could join us," she said as she took coats and hung them in a hall closet. "Wow, it looks like you bought out the store with this wonderful filled basket. Thank you so much."

"We're fortunate people," Daniel Elwyn said. "It's the least we could do."

Samantha introduced her grandparents to Gray's sister.

Suzanne smiled and urged them into the living room where the hearth was ablaze and the aroma was sweet with a crackling fruitwood fire. There were at least forty people in the room, but Samantha was quick to find Gray, his very noticeable chestnut hair gleaming in the glow of the fire's light. As she enjoyed watching him, he turned and his eyes became fastened to hers. He excused himself from the people he had been talking with and made his way toward Samantha.

"Hi," he said. "Did you come alone?"

"No. Gram and Gramp are here. Over there, talking to some people they know."

"Okay. Good. What can I get you to drink?"

"What are my choices?"

"Just about anything you could think of. Other than the traditional things, we also have a punch my father made. It's not bad, cranberry juice and a few additives."

"Additives, huh? The kind of additives that knock you out and you wake up in the morning wondering where you are?"

"Maybe. Want some?" he asked with a devilish smile.

Samantha laughed. "Why not? My grandparents won't let the big bad wolf get me."

Gray smiled and walked with her toward the punch bowl on the dining room table. "Don't be so sure. Your grandparents like me."

"Ah, so you admit you're a big bad wolf."

Gray poured the punch for her and placed the glass cup in her hands, his fingers brushing hers. "I'm glad you came," he said. "I've missed you."

Samantha felt a lump in her throat. She thought how uncomfortable it would be for them both if she showed any signs of emotional tears. She coughed slightly to cover up the moisture she felt accumulating in her eyes. "Must be the smoke from the fire," she said.

Gray looked at her beautiful eyes and then touched her hair where it rested against her back. "You look like a Christmas package," he said. "How about if you be mine?"

Samantha sipped her punch and smiled. "I don't know. What do I get in return?"

Gray leaned into her, his breath warm at her neck. "Whatever you want," he said.

As they stood, close enough to feel the warmth from one another's bodies, an attractive young woman walked up to Gray and seized his right arm. "Hey," she said, "I think you owe me some private time, don't you?" And then she leaned over toward Samantha and smiled as she said, "You don't mind if I steal him, do you?"

Gray looked down into Samantha's eyes. She glanced at the girl, at Gray, and then took a step back. "I should go and see how my grandparents are doing," she said.

As the young woman with a definite swing in her hips walked away with Gray, Samantha felt angry with herself for not having some witty reply on the tip of her tongue. She minded very much that he had been stolen away.

After her punch had been enjoyed and the cup placed on a kitchen tray, Samantha walked around the room saying hello to people she didn't recognize and some that she did. At one point, Irene Grayson walked to where Samantha stood looking at a family portrait and offered her a selection of tiny pastries.

"I'm very glad you could come and be with us this evening, Samantha. Suzanne told me that you and your grandparents have brought us a very generous basket for the food pantry. I can't tell you how appreciative we are for that. It's so needed."

"We're happy to help," Samantha said. "In fact, it was kind of fun picking out the variety of non-perishables. There's certainly an endless assortment to choose from."

"There is," Irene Grayson agreed with a smile. "Now where's that son of mine? He was anxiously waiting for you to arrive, and here you are alone. What's he doing?"

Samantha felt an adrenalin rush. Gray had been waiting for

her to arrive? She looked around for him and saw him talking with another couple about her parents' age, the young woman at his side. Irene Grayson followed Samantha's gaze and then whispered to her, "Go get him."

Samantha smiled as Gray's mother moved away, offering the sweets to other guests, and then she decided to make her move. Edging past several other people, she positioned herself slightly behind and next to Gray, then gently poked him in the ribs. He turned and looked at her with surprise, then smiled and said, "Hi there."

Samantha kept her facial expression serious. "You don't mind if I borrow Gray do you?" she said to his attractive companion, and then she tugged on his sleeve and urged him to follow her out toward the hallway.

"What's this?" he asked with a smile. "I think I like being fought over by two pretty females."

"Really?" Samantha said. "Well don't get used to it. I have a life among other men too, you know."

"Oh, yes," Gray said replacing the smile on his face with a very stern look. "Such as Will?"

"Yes, Will would be one of them," Samantha said with her hands clasped together behind her back.

"And are they all gay?" Gray asked.

"What?"

"Are the others gay too?"

"What are you talking about?" Samantha asked, her hands now clenched into tight fists at her side.

"Sam," Gray said as he placed his hands on her arms, "I was crushed when your friend Will showed up and danced your feet off that night. I wanted to sock the guy. But then I stopped in at your grandparents and, noting my vast depression over the man in your life, Molly told me that Will is an old college friend who happens to be gay. I can't tell you how happy I was to hear that."

Samantha looked down at her shoes and then up into his face. "I'm kind of glad that I worried you."

"Thanks," he said with a smile. "First you let the cat eat my food then you manage to taunt me with a guy who looks like he just hopped out of a magazine ad for fine Italian suits. Great."

Samantha laughed.

"Where is your little flea bag anyway?"

Samantha raised her eyebrows and opened her mouth. "How

dare you call Lucy a flea bag? I'm very attentive to her, she has no fleas. She's here in Plymouth with me for the holidays. I keep her in my room most of the time so she won't escape."

"My apologies to Lucy. So, you're here for the holidays now? Will you go to the Holly Stroll with me?"

"They still do that here?"

"Absolutely, every year, always on the twenty-second of December. That's just a few nights away. Will you come with me?"

Samantha smiled. "I've never been. When I was a kid, I was always looking out at the group holding the candles, wishing I could join in. It was all adults, of course, but I promised myself that one day I'd be a part of it all. I've been caroling though."

"Well, I haven't been caroling because if I sing someone will put tape over my mouth. I get too loud. So, come with me to the Holly Stroll. It's beautiful, and I promise not to sing."

"Okay," she said. "I'd love to."

As they stood together in the darkened hallway, Molly and Dan Elwyn walked toward them. "This has been lovely, John. Gray," Molly corrected herself. "I'm very pleased that you thought to invite the three of us. Samantha's folks are going to arrive in a couple of days. You should come by the house. We have lots of goodies stashed away and you know you're very welcome at our home anytime."

Gray smiled and reached out for Molly's hands. "Thank you. I'll be by. And Samantha has agreed to accompany me on the Holly Stroll."

Molly looked at her beaming granddaughter. "That sounds like a very Christmasy thing to do," she said. "We did it years ago, but these days we find the comfort of a blazing fire and a cup of warm cider to be more to our liking. You're welcome to come in after the stroll, although I think most people end up at a pub or something for a festive drink. Well, you do whatever you wish, you know you're always invited."

They said their goodnights and Gray helped Samantha into her coat, pulling at the lapels so that she was drawn near to him. "I'll see you very soon," he said, and then he watched as the three of them left his parents' house. He stood at the opened door, allowing the cold air to drift in until his father came up behind him and said, "Pretty gal you've got there, but let's not try heating the frigid outside, shall we?"

Samantha slipped into the backseat of her grandparents' car and hugged herself against the cold, wishing it was Gray who embraced her. This, she thought, is going to be a very special Christmas. Her parents would be there, her brothers would fly in from California, and then there was John Eldon Grayson, the icing on her Christmas cake.

"Did you have a good time, Sweetie?" Molly Elwyn asked from the front seat.

Samantha smiled in the dark. "I had a very good time. How about you two?"

"I had a great time," Dan Elwyn offered. "That punch had a good kick to it; I'll have to get that recipe."

Molly laughed. "And you're driving us home? I'm not so sure how secure we should feel, Samantha."

"Oh, I didn't have all that much," Dan said. "I had lots of good food and coffee too. Don't worry, I'm solid."

Molly turned around to give Samantha a smile. "Well, I thought it was a wonderful afternoon and early evening. They're a gracious family, and, of course, your Gray is a complete dream boy."

Samantha laughed. "He's not exactly *my* dream boy," she said, and in her thoughts she added *yet*. Gray represented everything she could have imagined in a man. He was handsome, charming, intelligent, completely appealing. In the past, she would have backed away believing that he was too good to be true, but something this time was telling her to go ahead. If I dare to love him and lose him, she thought, I will have known great love in my life, and the memory of that, I will treasure always.

The following day was Monday and, while her grandparents settled into their normal lives and Lucy slept contentedly on the soft bed, Samantha decided on a walk after breakfast. She was looking for a few select gifts; it crossed her mind that she would love to find a little something for Gray.

The streets of Plymouth were like a scene from a Christmas card. The old-fashioned lanterns were decked in holly and boxwood, and one large spruce tree right in the town's center was covered in red bows. It made Samantha wonder how that tree had been decorated, every bow spaced perfectly apart from the others. She could smell the mixed aromas of coffee from the local shops, balsam from the sale of trees, and chocolate from a local candy maker. It was cheerfully divine and confirmed even more the reality that this was the place she wanted to call home.

Having purchased additional gifts of slippers, pajamas and robes for her grandfather and her brothers, Samantha grasped the bulky packages and decided she needed a hot coffee. As she sat down with a steaming mug, she looked up and saw Gray's smiling face.

"Good morning," he said. "Now how did you know that this is my favorite coffee shop?"

Samantha smiled as he sat down with his own cup of coffee in a paper container.

"I don't suppose you'd believe me if I denied knowing," she said.

"Nope. You like me too much for this to be a simple coincidence. Who told you, my mother?"

Samantha laughed. "You're so arrogant. No one told me. My senses told me. I could smell the coffee and it beckoned me inside."

Gray lowered his head and raised his chestnut colored eyebrows. "My mother didn't have a hand in this?"

"Why would she?" Samantha asked as she blew gently at the hot coffee.

Gray squirmed a bit. "Well, let me see, maybe because she thinks you're pretty hot stuff."

"Really? What about you`? Do you think that too?"

"Now who's arrogant?" he asked with a smile.

Samantha looked very serious. "Well, fair's fair. So, you come here for coffee on a regular basis?"

"If I'm in town, I'm here every morning just about this time. I get to the point where it's around eleven o'clock and breakfast is just a memory. I'm not ready for lunch, so coffee fills the gap. Speaking of lunch, could you meet me in about two hours? I see you've been shopping. Will that timing work for you?"

"Yes, I think so. Where should we meet?"

"Well," he began, "have you ever had lunch on a tour boat?"

Samantha looked surprised. "No."

"Well then, you should meet me at the tour boats where we first met. They're anchored there for winter repairs and a general freshening up, but I can have the cabin warmed and I can pick up some lunch for us. What do you like? Sandwiches of some sort? Or Thai food?"

Samantha smiled. "Surprise me," she said.

Gray stood and picked up his container of coffee. "You've got it. I'm sorry I have to go; I'm meeting a client in ten minutes at my office, but will one-thirty work for you?"

"Sure," she said, and then he smiled at her and walked out of the cafe.

Samantha sat there sipping the warm brew, enjoying looking around at the hand-painted mural covering the walls. It was a colorful place and the coffee was wonderful. Within ten minutes of his leaving, Samantha gathered her packages together and headed out into the cold. As she passed an antique store, she decided to go in, leaving her bulky packages at the front desk. She wandered around finding some antique spoons she liked and thought her grandmother would enjoy using, and then she found silver napkin rings, each one different, very Victorian, which she liked for herself. She selected ten spoons for her grandmother and six napkin rings to put away for the future. As she looked at other items, she found a small sterling silver pin, a seahorse, and decided that it was the perfect gift for her mother. For her father, she decided that a wonderful box of chocolates would suit him best, filling the needs of his incessant sweet tooth.

As Samantha made her way toward the checkout counter, she stopped to look at a framed black and white photo. It was a picture of a tour boat, one of the very boats that Gray was overseeing, and the caption read that the man in the photo was the owner and Captain, Joseph Porter, Gray's elderly friend. This was it, the perfect gift for Gray. She took it down from the wall and, with her other great finds, she paid for them and then headed back to her grandparents' home before meeting Gray for lunch.

"Goodness," Molly said as Samantha dragged her purchases into the kitchen, "you've had a good time shopping, haven't you?"

Samantha smiled. "It was the best. I found really good things I think. I just need to get Dad's gift. I decided on a huge box of chocolates from that nice shop on Court Street. I'll get it in a couple of days. Oh, and I'll need to get a catnip mouse for Lucy of course."

"Of course," Molly said with a smile. "Want some lunch, Honey? I was just going to make a couple of tuna fish sandwiches."

"Oh, thanks, but I ran into Gray at a coffee shop and he invited me for lunch at one-thirty. I hope you don't mind."

"Mind?" Molly asked with a loaf of homemade bread in her hands. "Of course not. Where are you going? There are so many choices in town now."

Samantha slipped out of her coat and hung it on a wall peg. "He's asked me to meet him on one of the tour boats. He's having the heat turned on in the cabin and he's bringing a picnic of sorts."

"That's very romantic," Molly said. "Goodness, that boy knows how to win over hearts, doesn't he? Gosh, he's cute, Sam."

Samantha stood and gathered her packages together. "He does seem to be. However, I think I'll run upstairs with these packages and check on Lucy. I'll be back in a few minutes."

"Wait," Molly said, "take our little Lucy some tuna. Here. She'll like this," she said as she handed a small dish with white tuna in it to her granddaughter.

Samantha smiled. "You're a wonderful cat great-grandmother," she said. "I'll be right back, Gram."

In her room, Samantha gave Lucy the tuna, put her packages in a large chair, and then selected a navy blue jersey to change into. She brushed her long hair, gave Lucy a quick kiss and encouraging talk, then left to go back downstairs.

"I hear you have a luncheon date," her grandfather said from his chair and from behind his book.

Samantha smiled. "Yes, I do, with Gray on one of the tour boats."

Dan Elwyn peeked around his book, his glasses perched at the end of his nose. "I heard. Sounds like fun."

"I'll be here for supper, Gramp. I'm not abandoning you, I promise," she said as she moved to kiss her grandfather's cheek.

"Ah," he said, "but will you be joining us alone? That's the question."

Samantha laughed. "I guess we'll see," she said as she left the living room and walked to the kitchen.

She took her coat from its peg and slipped her arms into it as her grandmother sliced the tuna sandwiches diagonally. She looked up at her pretty granddaughter and asked, "Are you off, Honey? Don't forget gloves and a scarf. There's a sea wind blowing out there. You don't want to catch a chill."

Samantha smiled as she pulled gloves onto her hands. "I'll be fine, Gram. And I doubt I'll be long; Gray must have work to do this afternoon. I'll see you shortly."

"If you want to invite him for dinner, feel free. It's a simple meal, meatballs, noodles and green beans. I have ice cream in the freezer and cookies in the jar. He's welcome to join us."

"I'll tell him," Samantha said with a smile.

On her walk toward the harbor Samantha felt the invigorating sea air clinging to her face and she could feel her hair being lifted in the breeze. With her gloved hands tucked into her pockets, she made her way to the pier where the boats were docked and saw that one of them had lights on board and even a tiny Christmas tree on its deck. She smiled, feeling a rush of pure joy in her heart for this amazing man. As she approached the boat, she hesitated, taking in the sweet adventure of it all. And then she saw him as he opened the cabin door and stood there, his hands on his hips, a smile on his handsome face, waiting for her.

Chapter Six

As Samantha walked within a few feet of the anchored vessel, Gray extended his right hand to her and she willingly placed her gloved right hand in his firm grasp. When he pulled her to the boat, her chest softly collided with his and, for one amazing moment, Gray's warm breath was felt on Samantha's chilled skin.

"I have a nice warm cabin in here," he said. "Come on, I'll start you off with my special eggnog."

Samantha smiled as she slipped out of her coat and gloves. "I hope this isn't some of that knock-out stuff," she said. "I've been snookered with that before."

Gray looked at her and smiled as she left her coat on a chair and accepted the warm drink. "Snookered? Is that a lady's term for getting bombed? And who took advantage of you? I'll seek them out. I'll slay that dragon."

"My father mixed and gave me the eggnog," she said with a smile and then took a sip of the creamy but potent brew. "Hmm, this is good. Rum?" she asked.

"And just the tiniest portion of brandy," he said as they sat down, each at the end of a small sofa.

"This is wonderful," Samantha began. "This cabin is so cozy and warm, and the view is spectacular. Thank you for this."

"My pleasure," he said as he watched her eyes scanning the harbor. "So, tell me what you've been doing? Are you ready for Christmas? And for the stroll you promised to accompany me on? That's tomorrow night, you know."

"I haven't forgotten," she said and smiled. "I'm actually dying to go. And as for what I've been doing, I guess a little of everything. I pretty much finished my shopping, and I've helped my grandmother with some baking. Mostly, I've been being incredibly lazy I think. It's great."

Gray offered his guest more eggnog and she declined. "I'm

going to do well to walk having had this much," she said and laughed. "So, how about you? Do you Christmas shop for your family?"

Gray placed his eggnog cup down on a small trunk he used for a coffee table. "Yup. I bought nice warm sweaters for everyone in my family, including my nephew. Of course he also gets those books of yours, which he's sure to love."

Samantha nodded. "I'll have to speak to my brothers about getting married and having kids."

Gray raised his ample eyebrows and asked, "What about you? Are kids in your future?"

"I hope so. But I'm the old-fashioned type, marriage before the carriage, and there's no one handing me a diamond. So, yes, in the future."

Gray shifted in his seat enough to lean forward for a brown bag. From it he took a container of coleslaw, tightly wrapped sandwiches, and a bag of potato chips. He placed everything on the trunk next to paper plates, napkins and forks. "I was thinking of Thai food, but decided that might be a better choice for dinner some evening. I made a pot of coffee before you arrived. Would you prefer something else? I have soft drinks and bottled water."

"The coffee smells good. I'd like that, please."

Gray stood and poured two mugs of steaming black liquid. "Cream? Sugar?"

"Sometimes yes and sometimes just black. This time I'll have it black, thank you."

Gray sat back down and passed her a sandwich. "I wasn't all that sure what you'd like so I did the vegetable and cheese route. They're filled with lettuce, mildly hot peppers, black olives and roasted red peppers, draped in two different kinds of cheese, one of them cheddar. I hope that's okay."

"It sounds perfect," Samantha said as she accepted the sandwich and began to unwrap it. "I love roasted red peppers, and any kind of cheese. Thank you."

Samantha sat and stole the occasional glance at Gray when she could. She was amazed at the complete feeling of comfort she had in being with him. He was new and exciting, but he was also like being with someone she knew well. When she least expected it, he turned and caught her watching him.

"This is probably one of the best things I ever thought to do," he said. "I've always loved this boat. Having you join me here for lunch is even better than I thought it would be."

"You haven't done this before?"

"Nope. Not with anyone. Once in a while Captain Joe would give us hands a cup of coffee or a doughnut, but not a meal of any kind. This is my first on board, but not the last, I'm sure."

Samantha took bites of her sandwich and helped herself to a few chips and a scoop of coleslaw. As she looked out to the water, everything seemed muted as the darkness of the afternoon began to engulf the harbor. Lights on shore twinkled and she thought what a pretty scene it all made, with just a touch of snow on the ground.

"Are you warm enough?" he asked as he offered a refill of coffee.

"It's heavenly in here," she said as she held her cup for him. "I could actually live on this boat."

Gray laughed. "Yeah, I used to think that too, and I suppose I could. But I've gotten pretty used to the comforts of home."

"You have your own place, right?"

"Yes and no," he said. "I'm into the renovation of an older home. In warmer weather, I sometimes stay there overnight after working on it for a while. But this time of year I seek out my old bedroom at my parents' house. I'm hoping for a spring finish; the place is pretty much everything I ever wanted in a home. I'll take you there sometime if you're interested."

Samantha smiled. "I'd love to see it."

Gray nodded and then stood to adjust the heat in the small cabin.

Samantha looked at her watch and found it was nearly four o'clock and growing dark outside. "I'm so comfortable here and I hate to leave, but I thought I'd be back home before now and I don't want to concern Gram and Gramps. I should probably go."

"Did you bring a cell phone? Or would you like to use mine? You could give them a quick call."

Samantha stood and stretched. "I didn't bring my phone, but if I could use yours, I'm sure it would ease their minds to hear from me."

Gray reached into his trouser pocket for his phone and as he looked at it, he grimaced. "It needs charging," he said. "Come on, I'll shut off the heat in here and we'll stop by your grandparents' before we end our date with a nice drink at The Salty Dog. Word is there's a guitarist there tonight, are you game?"

"Sure," she said as she slipped her arms into her coat. "I'm ready if you are."

Gray gave her a sly smile. "Ready for what?" he asked.

"I think we should go now," Samantha suggested with a smile. She wasn't falling for that loaded question. He was an incredible flirt and she wasn't going to let him get the best of her. Not yet.

With their coats, gloves and scarves in place, Gray flipped switches to turn off three small lights and then he helped Sam to navigate the step and unsteady motion of the boat against the pier. He closed the cabin door and locked it, and then with one last glance at the little Christmas tree on deck swaying in the wind, he joined Samantha on solid footing.

Samantha turned to look at the tiny lit tree and smiled. "This has been such fun; I love this kind of thing. Thank you, and lunch was terrific. It was all a treat. At the risk of arousing your arrogant side, I'll finish with the fact that you're amazing."

Gray laughed. "Well, of course I am." At that point, he took her hand in his and they walked toward his car.

With a stop first at her grandparents' home to say hello and all is well, they drove to The Salty Dog and selected a small round table in the corner.

"What will you have? Would you like a bite to eat and a cold drink, or a coffee?"

"Do they have cider here?"

Gray smiled. "Oh yes. Spiked or unspiked? Warm or cold?"

Samantha pulled her gloves off and slipped her arms out of her coat. "I'll have it warm and unspiked, thank you."

"Damn," he said to be amusing. "Guess I won't be getting away with anything tonight."

She gave him a stern look and then he turned toward the bar to place their order.

When the guitarist began to play, his music and mood reflected soft Spanish Classical, dreamy and soothing for a cold winter night. But then he moved from gentle tones to a more stimulating beat and eventually back to the softer melody, like the ebb and flow of the tide, one moment the waves rising and cresting, then crashing on shore only to withdraw the force and relax as it shifts from sand to rejoin the surf.

Samantha leaned back in her chair and folded her hands

across her lap, entranced with the music and the fine aromas wafting through the warm air of the room.

Gray placed two mugs of warm cider on their table then sat down next to her where he had a good view of the guitarist. During a low volume moment he asked, "Do you like dogs?"

Samantha took a sip of her cider and then laughed. "Where did that come from?"

"Just wondered," Gray said.

Samantha patted her lips with a napkin and looked at him. "I love all animals," she said.

"Oh, that's right. I nearly forgot that you were named for a hamster."

Samantha gave him another of her stern looks. "Sure you did. You're not going to ever forget that, I know you."

Gray laughed. "Well, I'm glad to hear you like dogs."

"Why?"

"Because I hope to have a dog one day. I like cats, mind you, but I had a dog as a kid and I've always wanted another. Do you think Lucy likes dogs?"

Samantha smiled. "I have no idea. I'll ask her. But why is it important to know if my cat likes dogs?"

Gray tilted his head and pursed his lips for a moment in thought. "I just thought it would be nice if your cat and my dog got along, but I think everything is about animals getting to know one another, just like us."

Samantha sipped her warm cider and, although she turned her head and attention back to the performer, she kept thinking about the question of merging their pets. What was he thinking?

When the music stopped as the guitarist took a break, Gray asked Samantha if she had good warm clothes for the Holly Stroll just twenty-four hours away.

"I do," she said. "I'll wear this coat because it's long and warm, and I'll wear slacks or jeans and a warm sweater."

"Maybe some long thermal underwear too," he said with a smile. "It's supposed to be pretty cold, down in the single digits."

"Are we out a long time?" she asked.

"Oh, maybe an hour to an hour and a half. It's more about seeing the historical houses along the main drag decorated for the holidays. The group usually starts with a couple of hundred enthusiastic people then, little by little, it dwindles down until you find yourself walking alone."

Samantha laughed. "Has that happened to you?"

Gray nodded. "Yup, to me and a handful of others, but it's fun."

"The stroll starts at seven?" she asked after a sip of cider.

"Seven, right. After that invigorating walk in the cold, most people stop in at a place like this, or go home for a hot drink of some sort I suppose."

"What do you do?"

Gray gestured to the room around him. "Before this became The Salty Dog this past year, it was almost strictly a coffee bar. A few of us would end up here for something to chase the chill. Someone in the crowd always had a flask of brandy to add discreetly to the coffee, of course."

Samantha smiled. "So, will we be coming back in here after our stroll?"

"Sure, if you'd like to."

The guitarist took his place again on a tall stool and the music began with the relaxing tones of Spanish Classical, melodies this performer seemed to favor.

After an hour or so there, Gray noticed Samantha checking her watch.

"It's just after six," he said. "Are you expected someplace?"

"Just at Gram and Gramp's. I told my grandmother I'd help her with a few things. She made these crispy little pickles today and she canned them for gifts. One of the things I do to help is cut circles of fabric to go over the top of each covered jar, and then I tie pretty ribbon around the lid to keep it all in place."

"Sounds nice," he said. "How many does she make?"

"About thirty jars," Samantha said with a smile. "She gives ten or so away as little gifts, but probably twenty of them go to a bake sale at church. She's amazing. I love the way my grandparents live. They aren't rich, but they're content and happy."

Gray shook his head. "That's important stuff. My parents live a decent life too; I like the way they handle themselves."

They were both quiet, thought-filled, their eyes fastened on the musician.

"What about you, Sam?" he asked out of the blue.

"Me? What about me?"

"How's your life? Are you happy with it as is?"

Samantha smiled and then looked into his beautiful and expressive eyes. "I think I'm in a good place. It's kind of like being on a journey. I'm part way there."

"How so?" he asked. "Explain more."

"Well," she said as she shifted in her chair, "I like living in Boston, but I know it's a stopping off place. I don't intend to stay there for much longer. As for my work, I love writing the children's books and I love working at the museum, but I think there's more to do." She laughed as she pulled gloves on over her fingers. "I must sound restless, but that's not so. It's just that I want some things more. I want a nice family; I had parents who were wonderful but absent a good deal of the time. I want to be a parent who's there. I want a comfortable little home, nothing pretentious, just a place to be at ease."

"And someone to love and be loved by."

"And someone to love and be loved by," she repeated his words.

Gray took a long look at her beautiful face then asked, "Should we go so that you can help Molly with those pickles?"

"We should," she said.

Gray stood and helped Samantha into her coat then slipped his own coat on, draping his scarf loosely in place. They pushed their chairs toward the table's center and then walked out of the warm room and into the cold night. His car was parked on the street and he opened her door then stood aside for her to seat herself. Noticing her fasten the seat belt, he walked around to the driver's side.

"I feel lazy," she said as he started the engine. "I could easily walk from here."

"No way," he said. "It's dark and cold; I'm delivering you home to your family. When are your parents arriving? And your brothers?"

"Mum and Dad will be here on the morning of the twenty-fourth, but the twins should be here the day after tomorrow, the twenty-third. Kyle had to work right up until an hour before they were leaving for the airport, and Peter was doing some last minute shopping from what he told Gram. It'll be fun; I love it when we can all get together. It doesn't happen every year."

Gray maneuvered the car away from the curb and began to drive toward the Elwyn home. As he pulled up in front of the house, he smiled and commented on the warmth emitting from lights at the windows. "It looks so inviting," he said.

"And," Samantha began, "you're invited to come in with me now, or anytime you wish. Personally, I think Molly Jane Elwyn has a crush on you."

Gray smiled and shifted the car into park. "I'm glad to hear it," he said. "How about her gorgeous granddaughter? Any crush going on in her head?"

In her head and heart, Samantha wanted to say. "I think you should come in and say hello. I'll bet there's hot coffee or cocoa in there."

"It's very tempting," he said, "but there are some final touches I need to address on the blueprints for a restaurant. I think I'd better get that task finished so that I can go out with you tomorrow and have a great evening without feeling guilty. I promised these folks I'd have the plans completed by Christmas."

"A man of your word," she teased.

"I am," he said.

"Okay, then," Samantha said as she placed her hand on the car door's latch. "I'll talk to you tomorrow I expect. Would you like me to meet you someplace before the stroll?"

Gray started to get out of the car to open her door.

"Oh, don't," she said, "I'm perfectly fine opening this door; it's cold out there, stay put. But as for tomorrow evening, I could meet you if you'd like."

"No," Gray said firmly as he sat back in his seat. "I'll pick you up about six forty-five. We'll park down town where the stroll begins and, later, we'll decide what we want to do to warm up."

"Okay," she said, "I can't wait. Goodnight, Gray."

As she began to move toward the partially opened door, Gray reached for her hand and applied just a touch of affectionate pressure. "Night, Sam," he said.

Inside, before Samantha hung her coat in the hallway closet, she tucked the gloves in the coat's pockets and then walked into the aromatic kitchen.

"Wow," she said to her grandmother, "it sure smells like pickles in here. I love them; they're so crispy and delicious. Are we ready to decorate their tops?"

Molly smiled and dried her wet hands on her apron. "They're all ready for you: thirty-six jars of them. Your grandfather has laid claim to two jars and, of course, I'll save a jar for both you and John."

Samantha smiled and washed her hands before beginning to select the pretty pieces of material with which she would cover the jars. "He'll appreciate that and so will I." Samantha then added, "Since most people refer to him as Gray, have you considered doing the same?"

"I should," Molly began, "I know. As a boy, he was John Grayson, so it's second nature to call him John, but I agree, everyone else calls him Gray. I'll try."

Samantha laughed. "I'm sure he doesn't mind being called John; it's just that every time you say his name, I have to go through this translation process and change John to Gray. It's not really a big deal."

Molly turned to look at her granddaughter. "You really like him, don't you?"

Samantha could feel a flush of pink at her cheeks. "He's very nice," she said.

Molly chuckled. "Nice? That isn't a word I would have used to describe John Grayson. He's what most would call a stud muffin."

Samantha laughed out loud.

"What?" Molly began. "Do you think I was born old? And, after all, my eyes still work perfectly fine. He's yummy."

Samantha laughed again. "Better not let Gramps hear you say that; he'll be jealous."

Molly laughed. "Nah, he's used to me drooling over Paul Newman. Now, let's use these saucers as patterns to cut the rounds of material for the jars. I'll cut, you place them on and tie the ribbons. How's that sound?"

"Easy," Samantha said cheerfully.

"So," Molly began as she sat at the kitchen table across from her granddaughter, "you're going off on the Holly Stroll tomorrow evening."

Samantha smiled. "Yes, I'm excited about it. It seems like a very festive thing to do. The day we went to the Grayson's party for the food pantry, you said that you and Gramps went years ago. After, did you go out for a drink or did you come back home to warm up?"

"We always came back home, usually with a few others invited as well. We were hot cocoa people, although a couple of them, including your grandfather, would add a touch of something stronger to the chocolate. I enjoyed those times, but now, well, there's something ever so nice about a blazing fire and a soft chair." Molly smiled at Samantha and continued to cut circles out of pretty fabric. "You and Gray are young, you'll have fun."

"What about Mum and Dad? Did they ever take the Holly Stroll?"

Molly shook her head. "No, the stroll was introduced here in town about twenty years ago. By then your parents were married and often out to sea on their exploratory voyages. I really love it that they come home once in a while now for the holidays. It's nice for us and it's nice for you kids. And I think it's nice for your mother and father as well. It just makes everything seem right."

Samantha continued to work, carefully centering the circles of pretty material over the jar covers. She thought about how lonely it must have been for her grandparents to lose their only child to a life on the sea. It was Samantha who seemed to have the strongest family ties, staying in Massachusetts, wanting to make her home in Plymouth. Even her adventuresome brothers had made their way to sunny California without a thought for being missed or missing anyone in particular.

"You know, Sam," Molly said as if reading her granddaughter's mind, "you're the glue that holds this family together. I'm not sure we'd all be gathering if it weren't for you. I'm very grateful. I love the preparation before they all arrive and then I am in pure glory when they're here. One thing my son did right was marry your mother. She's a lovely daughter-in-law, never had a single doubt about the two of them together."

Sam thought about what her grandmother had said. She'd wished as a child that her parents were at home more but, over the years, she had learned to accept what was. Having them home when possible was wonderful and it was understood that these times were to be treasured and accepted. "I'm so glad they'll all be here this year, Gram. I think about Peter and Kyle sometimes, that when they have wives and families of their own, especially if they remain in California, it won't always be possible for them to come here. I just want this time around to be filled with joy. I'm anxious to see each one of them."

Molly smiled as she cut her circles. "Me too," she said.

Then with a quick glance to Samantha she asked, "Were you lonely as a little one?"

Samantha looked up at her grandmother. "No, I don't think so. I didn't know any difference. My best times, though, were here. We were all together and it was usually a time for celebrating or it was relaxing summer. I always knew that I wanted a different life, a life with consistency. Once I buy a house of my own, I want to stay there, just like you and Gramps have. I want roots."

Molly looked at her granddaughter's beautiful face. She was luminous but had a little glimmer of sadness in her eyes. "I think you'll have all that, Sam. That's your goal and you're an achiever. Your dad and mom found their lives on the sea. There's nothing wrong with that, but there's not a lot of time for hearth and home either. The way we live here in Plymouth is exactly the way I always thought about living. It suits us."

"It suits me too," Samantha said, fastening on the last bow.

Chapter Seven

Samantha woke up on December twenty-second thinking happily that this was the day of Plymouth's Holly Stroll. She smiled at Lucy who gently pawed at her friend's long hair and then she told the attentive cat all about the coming evening. "You can watch out through this window," Samantha explained as she gestured to her right. "You'll see part of it, Lucy, but believe me when I tell you that you wouldn't want to go. You'd be frightened, and it's cold. I'll tell you all about it when I get home." At that point, Samantha swung her legs from beneath the warm covers and slid her feet into soft slippers. After a quick trip into the washroom, Samantha rinsed and filled Lucy's water bowl and left her a dish of her favorite kibble. With her robe half on, maneuvering her left arm into a long sleeve, she was careful to close her bedroom door and then made her way downstairs to the warm kitchen where the mixed aromas of coffee and Danish pastry filled the air.

"Hi, Gram," Samantha cheerfully greeted her grandmother who was standing at the stove stirring a sweet sauce. "What's this for?" she asked as she gently kissed her grandmother's left cheek.

"My rum cake. When this thickens up a bit, I'll add the rum. When it's cooled, I'll poke holes in my nice cake and drizzle this potent mix on and through it. It's your mother's favorite topped with whipped cream. What would you like for breakfast, Sweetie?"

"Did I smell your Danish?"

Molly laughed. "Of course you did. Your grandfather already treated himself to two pieces. Help yourself; it's under that foil on the counter. There's tea, coffee and orange juice too."

Samantha moved around the kitchen fetching a small plate

for the Danish and a cup for her tea. "Where's Gramps?" she asked as she sat down at the round table.

"He went downtown to pick up the paper and more butter. I always underestimate the butter needed. When I saw him slathering it on his Danish this morning, I knew I was in trouble. Anyway, he'll be back soon. Oh, and when you go back upstairs, I have a little treat for Miss Lucy. I had a couple of slices of roast beef left over and thought she'd like that. I cut it up into tiny bits."

Samantha smiled with a bite of the delicious Danish in her mouth. "I keep telling Lucy how lucky she is to have a Great Grandmother who is so kind to her. She'll enjoy the roast beef. At my place, she eats a little of what I have, along with her own food."

Molly smiled at Samantha. "They're such good companions," she said. "So, tonight's the stroll. Are you excited?"

"Very. Gray said to dress warm so I thought I'd wear my gray flannel slacks; they're warmer than jeans. I also have a nice black sweater – it's long and warm. That under my heavy coat, with gloves and a hat, I should be all set."

"And are you going out later for a hot drink?"

"Gray said we would."

"That sounds like a nice evening. You have your key if you get home late. Would you like me to do anything with Lucy?"

Samantha swallowed a sip of her tea. "Not unless you want to stop in and give her a few pats. I'll feed her before I go."

"Poor little thing," Molly said. "I wonder if she's lonely."

"I don't think so. She's alone frequently when I'm working. I think she likes it here where she can look out the windows at the birds. In Boston she sees mostly pigeons flittering from one ledge to another. Here, the tiny birds seem to amuse her."

"I'm glad; I'd hate to think she was lonely or bored here."

Samantha finished her Danish pastry and licked frosting from her left thumb as her grandfather walked into the kitchen. "Hey there, Sunshine," he said to his granddaughter. "Nice to see that bright little face of yours. Aren't those the best Danish pastries you ever had? I think I might just have another with a good cup of coffee."

Molly turned around from where she stood at the stove. "Daniel Elwyn, a banana or a Clementine might be a better choice."

With a smile and a wink at Sam, her grandfather poured himself a cup of coffee and sought out another pastry. "Isn't it cute the way she worries about me?" he asked.

Samantha laughed and then sipped her tea. "If this keeps up, you'll need to make more of those pastries, Gram."

"I'll need to anyway. Everyone expects them for Christmas breakfast, along with the waffles and eggs, and, of course, the tray of fresh fruit. Goodness, we sure do eat a lot at the holidays, don't we?"

"It's all your fault, Molly," Dan said with a twinkle in his eye. "If you weren't such a good cook, we wouldn't devour so much."

"Sure, blame me," she countered in good humor.

With the new day ahead of her, Samantha asked if there was something she could do to help. When both of her grandparents said they had everything under control, Sam decided to go to her room where she could do two things at once, keep Lucy company and begin an outline for her new book. This one, she decided, would be about Lucy the cat who made friends with a bright red Cardinal, a Christmas bird.

By two in the afternoon when she hadn't surfaced for lunch, Dan Elwyn knocked on her door and asked if she'd like a sandwich.

"Okay," she agreed, "that sounds good." Quickly, Samantha, who was still in her pajamas and robe, replaced those bed clothes with jeans and a tan jersey. She brushed her long hair, gave Lucy a few more of her favorite snacks, told her she'd be back soon, then went downstairs to Molly's kitchen.

"Hi, Sweetie," Molly greeted as she sat at the kitchen table across from her husband of more than fifty years. "I made you a chicken sandwich with cranberry sauce and a bit of stuffing. I hope that's still a favorite of yours."

"Oh, yes," Samantha said as she poured herself a glass of water from a pitcher in the refrigerator. "I feel so spoiled here. At home, I eat whatever I can find. It's no fun cooking for yourself."

"What do you eat?" Dan asked with a napkin blotting the corners of his mouth.

Samantha shook her head. "Sometimes I eat cheese and crackers. Sometimes I run out of cheese and then I eat just crackers." She looked up to two horrified faces.

"But then sometimes I eat fruit. I like grapes and apples. And I cook an egg now and then, and toast." She looked at her grandparents who were not impressed.

Dan Elwyn shook his head. "I think you need to move down here where we can keep an eye on you, young lady."

Molly smiled at her granddaughter. "I know you can cook, I've seen it for myself. It's just not fun if there isn't someone around to say how good it is, right?"

"Right," Samantha agreed, and then she drank the last of her water.

"Have you started a new book?" Molly asked.

"Yes. It's about Lucy and a Cardinal. I'm really on a roll about this one. It will be a Christmas story and, if all goes well, it may be out next year just about this time. I'm really excited about it."

"That's wonderful," Dan Elwyn said. "Well, don't let us hold you up. Go back to it while it's fresh in your mind."

"Okay, but are you sure there's nothing I can do to help? I wouldn't mind at all; I can easily pick up the story later."

"Go," Molly urged. "There isn't a single thing you need to do down here. We'll have a little supper around five-thirty. Just enough to tide you over for that invigorating walk through town. I know you won't want much after having a late lunch, but I have some nice chowder. Maybe that would appeal to you before going out into the cold."

"Sounds great," Samantha said as she took her plate and cup to the sink before going back upstairs to a sleeping cat and the bones of her work.

When the doorbell rang that evening, Samantha was in her coat and ready to go. She opened the door to Gray who eyed her from head to toe and smiled. Then seeing Molly and Dan, he greeted them and asked them if they'd care to join the stroll. When they laughed and declined, he promised to take good care of their granddaughter.

"I wouldn't let her out of here with you if I thought you wouldn't take the best care of her," Dan Elwyn said with a smile.

Gray took Samantha's hand and led her to his warm car where he opened the door for her. "You look warm and wonderful," he said before closing the door and going to the driver's side. They parked downtown near to the courthouse where the stroll began. They found at least one hundred people standing around, some with lanterns, some with flashlights or candles. It was exciting and festive.

"I love this," she said as she watched the crowd thicken with more people.

"Me too. I like to squeeze every ounce of the holidays out where it can be completely enjoyed. This year," he said with an intent look to his companion, "is going to be the best stroll yet. I can feel it."

Samantha felt a chill as she surveyed his handsome face. This was possibly dangerous territory, but she was glad to be going anyway. Gray was simply irresistible and perhaps a tempting Christmas gift to herself.

"All set?" he asked as he reached for his door handle.

"Yes," she replied with her hand at the door. As she began to open it, Gray was there, pulling the door and her toward him.

The gathering was merry, people were laughing, and as they approached a few people nodded and said good evening to Gray and Samantha, visually, a handsome couple.

The walk began within moments, a flurry of last minute arrivers hurrying to join the group. They walked, their guide pointing out historical residences and places of business along the way, explaining the relevance of each Christmas decoration to the people who lived or worked in that place. It was interesting as well as fun. Samantha found it especially intriguing when they came to the Joshua Crowell House where the entire seventeenth century family had made their living sewing draperies, bed linens, feather-filled pillows and even some upholstered furniture. The well-lit decoration on that home's door was a quilted, stuffed heart and stems of bright berried holly.

The night was cold but invigorating; Samantha loved it all.

When the evening's stroll was through and they were back at the courthouse, Gray walked with Samantha to his car. "Might I interest you in a hot drink?"

"Absolutely," she said with a shiver.

"And do you have a preference for where?"

"No. Do you?"

"I do. I'd like to show you my house. We can light a fire

and I do have a couple of comfortable chairs and some pretty decent stuff to make us a nice drink. Are you game?"

"Sure," she said as a chill went through her body. "I'd love to see your house and the fire sounds great."

Gray started the engine and put the car into drive. A brief ride to a street just blocks away from the courthouse brought them to a stop and a house where a lantern light welcomed them to the front door. "This is it," Gray said as they walked from the car. He inserted a key into the lock and they stepped inside to an entryway less than warm. Gray ushered Samantha into the parlor and immediately put a match to the prepared hearth. Within moments, the flames leapt into the chimney and the smell of maple logs burning filled the room with warm air.

"Let me take your coat," he said. "Sit near to the hearth; it'll warm you to the extent you'll want to move away after a bit." He pulled the two chairs closer and Samantha sat down.

"This is wonderful," she said. "This house is fantastic. When did you buy it?"

"About three years ago. I've been poking and prodding at it ever since. It's nearly there; I can't wait to live here. I have a new furnace going in next month; the electric and the roof have been completely redone, it's in good shape except for some paint and wallpaper, and some furniture of course. Now for that drink. I have Coke, I have white and red wine, I have brandy, and I can make us a mixed drink if you prefer."

"Got any hot cocoa?" Samantha asked.

Gray laughed as he stood with his right hand on his right hip. "No, I'll have to remember to stock that. I have tea and coffee. How about if I make you my special?"

"Dare I ask what that is?" Samantha asked with a smile.

"Nope, it's a secret."

Samantha made a frowning face. "Hmm, okay, I guess I'll try it. You have aroused my curiosity."

Gray stoked the fire and smiled before he went to the kitchen. He came back in just a few minutes, handing to Samantha a warm stemmed glass filled with a garnet liquid.

"This is pretty," she said and then she sniffed at the rim before taking a sip.

Gray watched her, enjoying the way the light from the fire played against her amber hair.

"Oh," she said, "this is too good. What is it?"

"My version of Sangria," he said. "I mix a bit of wine, a bit of brandy, a bit of orange juice and ginger ale, warm it up, and here we are."

Samantha took a few more sips. "This is delicious. I'm fearful I could become too fond of this."

Gray smiled and took a long sip of his drink. "I'm glad you like it. When we've warmed up a little, I'll take you on a tour of the house."

"If I can walk," Samantha teased. "This stuff is potent."

They talked about the house, its view of the harbor from the front parlor and two of the upstairs bedrooms. They talked of who had lived there before, a town legislator first and then a publisher of a small town newspaper. It was interesting to look around and imagine the life one lived there with no electricity and only the heat from the hearth's flames to take away the winters' cold.

"This is incredibly comfortable and toasty," she said, "but I'd love to see the rest of the house if you're ready."

Gray stood and held out a hand to her. "Right this way," he said as he led her to a spacious dining room and, beyond that, a kitchen that would thrill any cook. Copper pans hung over a center island where a well-used thick piece of wood lay, ready for the preparation of meals.

"This is outstanding," Samantha said. "Did you do this?"

"I actually haven't had to touch the kitchen," Gray said. "Even the copper utensils were here. It's rustic, but I like it. The stove and frig were new to the former owners about five years ago. I have no quarrel with them; they work fine, so I plan to use them as is. Come on, let's move on."

He led her to a room at the back of the house, small and lined with what could be book shelves, and then to another small room off the kitchen, a pantry. Next to the pantry, Samantha viewed a small but adequate bathroom.

"There's a stairway for the front of the house and another for the back," he said as he flipped a switch to illuminate the stairway from the kitchen area hall. With a gentle hand to the small of her back, Gray urged Samantha upstairs where there were four ample bedrooms and a large bathroom with a deep, claw-foot tub.

"This is fantastic," she said. "I love the slanted walls, and the wide pine flooring. I have no doubt why you love this place,

Gray. It's completely charming."

Gray looked at her, his hands on his hips, his thumbs looped into his belt. "Yeah, I like it."

Samantha walked to a front window. "I'll bet the view from here is great by daylight. I can see little lights from boats in the harbor."

"The view is good," he said. "It's one of the reasons I wanted this house. I actually knew the people who once lived here. When I was a kid, I had a paper route and I delivered to these folks. They were nice, happy people. The vibes here are good."

Samantha smiled. "I like that." She reached out and touched a wall briefly. "Good energy floating around," she said.

"Let's go back down and enjoy the fire and our drinks," he said. "It's cold up here."

Samantha took one last look from the window toward the harbor, then turned and walked with Gray out of the room and down the front stairs. Gray walked to the hearth and stirred the remaining wood, encouraging it to provide a bit more heat and gentle light.

"Am I seeing you at Christmas?" he asked as he sat in the chair next to Samantha.

She hesitated and looked from the flames to his eyes. "Do you want to?"

Gray gave her a slow smile. "Very much so, but I also know you have limited time with your family and I don't want to interrupt."

"You wouldn't be. They all like you and I'm sure they'd enjoy seeing you again. You know how my grandparents feel about you; you're always welcome."

"Okay, so your family would probably approve, how about you? How does Samantha feel about seeing me on Christmas?"

She sipped her drink and gave him a flirty smile. "Well, I guess I could work you into my schedule. Of course, I'd very much enjoy seeing you at Christmas. I assume you're dining with your family."

"Oh, yes. I'm in charge of an appetizer and the salad. We plan on dinner at two, what about you? Do you have a time for when you'll sit down to a meal?"

"We usually have dinner around four. We munch on things that are bad for us as we open gifts and sit around looking at one another's treasures. Four o'clock may seem late to eat, but that's what we do I'm afraid. Would you like to join us for dessert? By five or six, surely you'd be ready to enjoy some sweets."

"I would," he said. "So I'll plan on seeing you after five."

Samantha nodded as she swallowed the last of her drink.

"What do you do on Christmas Eve?" he asked.

"I'm not sure yet. Sometimes we go to midnight Mass, sometimes we're just too lazy and get into our pajamas early. I kind of leave that up to Mom and Dad. What about you?"

"It's a night of food preparation until around ten. After that, we sometimes go off to church as you mentioned, but there are times when everyone is just too tired. Suzanne and her family arrive before midnight, with Michael sound asleep of course. The morning is a bit chaotic with Santa's presents being ripped open." He laughed and shook his head. "It's fun though, I'm not complaining. My sister arrives with sugar cookies and other goodies, so it's not a bad situation no matter what. I'd love to see you, but you have a hefty schedule with your family arriving. I'll look forward to your grandparents' home on Christmas Day. Speaking of your grandparents', I should probably get you back there."

Gray helped Samantha into her coat then slipped his arms into his own before making sure that the fire was completely out and the damper was closed.

Samantha smiled and nodded. "Okay," she said, and after he drove her home, she went to her room and slept soundly with Lucy snuggled at her shoulder.

Christmas Eve Day brought the entire family together. Samantha felt privileged and thrilled to be in their presence, everyone talking about where they'd been and what they'd been doing over the last few weeks since Thanksgiving. The atmosphere couldn't have been more filled with love and laughter, good food and interesting conversations.

"Where's that handsome Gray?" her mother asked. "I've heard he's in the picture."

"Can't imagine where you heard that," Samantha said with a wink to her grandmother.

"Wasn't me," Molly Elwyn said as she nodded toward her husband.

"Snitch!" he said.

Samantha laughed. "No secrets around this place. However,

he's coming over tomorrow for dessert. So, yes, he's in the picture."

After a few games of Scrabble, the entire family donned their coats and went off to midnight Mass. "I think I need church tonight," Mary Elwyn said. "Being out to sea, we miss these traditional things. It's good to go, it's what the holiday is all about after all."

Christmas morning Samantha opened her eyes to see Lucy pretty much in the same position she went to sleep in, at Samantha's shoulders. She reached a warm hand from beneath the covers to stroke the purring cat, said Merry Christmas to her, and then turned from her side to her back, allowing her eyes to scan the snow covered tree tops. Samantha smiled thinking about the day. It would all be fun, but seeing Gray later for dessert was something her heart longed for.

After breakfast, she would wrap his gift and place it beneath the tree with the others for her family. Without further hesitation, she slipped out of bed, pulled the covers in place then fetched Lucy's catnip mouse from the closet shelf. "There," she said, "and I'll save you a nice portion of Christmas dinner, Lucy, even mashed potato," which the cat loved loaded with sour cream.

Outside of her room, dressed in jeans and a red sweater, Samantha ran into her brother, Peter. "Hey," he said, "you trying to beat me to the Christmas tree and Santa's gifts?"

Samantha laughed. "Yeah, well I've been a very good girl; I'm not so sure about you though."

Peter gave her a long look before turning to race her downstairs.

"Good Lord," their father said as he stood motionless at the bottom, "will you two ever grow up?"

"Probably not," Peter admitted. "Where's the fun in that?"

Charles Elwyn smiled and shook his head as he continued on his quest for coffee in his mother's kitchen.

With the family gathered around the tree, a tray of pastries on the coffee table and everyone with either coffee or orange juice, they began to open their gifts. Kyle looked nostalgic as he opened a gift from his girlfriend back in California.

"That from Katie?" Molly asked as she noticed his quiet demeanor.

Kyle nodded. "Yeah, a wristwatch." He held it up for everyone to see then fastened it onto his wrist. "I'll call her later; it's too early out there just now."

"Why do I get the feeling this is getting serious?" Mary Elwyn asked.

"Because it is," Peter chimed in. "He's nuts about this girl. And I have to admit, she's worth it. He picked a good one."

Mary smiled and patted Kyle's shoulder. "I'm happy for you, Honey. I'll look forward to meeting her sometime."

As each gift was opened and shown around the room, food was enjoyed along with a warm fire. "This is just the way I like Christmas," Dan Elwyn said. "Couldn't be better."

Later, as they cleared the table of dinner's offerings, Samantha took tiny portions upstairs to Lucy, then changed from her jeans into a knee-length gray skirt and a silky blouse to match. She brushed her hair and made her way back downstairs when she heard the doorbell ring. Opening the door to a waft of cold air, she felt only warmth as her green eyes met those of her guest.

"Hi," he said. "Merry Christmas."

"Merry Christmas," she said as she took his coat and hung it in the hall closet.

"This is for you," he said as he took a small box from his pocket, then handed her a bottle of wine and a bouquet of white roses as well. "I thought your family might enjoy this cranberry wine made here in Plymouth, and the flowers are for Molly. I thought about bringing something for dessert but, knowing your grandmother, she probably has enough to feed the whole town."

Samantha smiled. "You have her pegged. Come on in. Gramp and Dad are in the parlor, Mum and Gram are in the kitchen; I think Kyle is talking on the phone with his California girlfriend, and Peter could be just about anywhere. Probably using his laptop to keep in touch with friends."

They stood in the hallway at the foot of the stairs. "Which direction would you care to go in?" she asked.

"Right here is good," he said as he leaned forward and left a gentle kiss on her lips.

Samantha backed up slightly not expecting that. "I have something for you too," she said. "I'll get it from under the tree; wait here and we can open our gifts before everyone comes along to greet you."

Gray stood still, a smile on his face as he watched her gracefully move into the parlor. When she returned, she handed him an oblong box and invited him to sit down on the carpeted stairs with her. "Open it," she said with a smile.

"How about if we open our gifts together?" he asked.

Samantha smiled, her left shoulder touching his right shoulder as they sat like children on the same stair tread.

Gray found the old photo of the tour boat and stared at it in disbelief for several moments. At the same time, Samantha lifted a gold chain from the small box and found, suspended from it, a beautiful carved shell.

"This is incredible," Gray said holding the framed photo. "Where in the world did you get this? I love it."

"I found it in an antique shop," she said with a smile. "But, Gray, this necklace, it's absolutely gorgeous. It looks hand carved."

"It is," he said as he helped her to secure it around her neck. "I carve shells as a hobby. I thought you might like the Mayflower design, and, if you look closer, you'll find your name riding one of the waves."

Samantha's eyes were fastened on the delicate piece, then she looked at him and smiled. "I'm amazed," she said. "This is the most beautiful gift I've ever received. Thank you, Gray." She leaned closer and their lips met briefly before Peter made his presence known at the top of the stairs.

When the visiting and desserts were enjoyed and it was getting late into the night, Samantha walked Gray to the door.

"I love this necklace, Gray. Thank you again."

He slipped his arms into his overcoat and then took her shoulders in his hands, bringing her closer to him. "You're welcome. I love my gift as well."

Samantha smiled and asked, "How many other women around here have these?" She lifted the shell from her chest to look at it closer then she looked to his eyes for the answer.

"Two," he said. "My mother and an elderly woman who loved my mother's shell. She asked me to do one for her."

Samantha leaned forward and kissed him next to his lips. Within moments, his lips claimed hers in a warmly locked embrace. The feel of him, her hands at his sides, her lips being teased and caressed, made her feel almost dizzy.

"I'll call you tomorrow," he said, and then he was gone.

Chapter Eight

Upon waking the day after Christmas, Samantha felt a little sad. She knew that her parents were leaving that evening to rejoin their ship near Bali. Kyle would be returning to California to see his girlfriend, and Peter was expected back to complete work on a project in Pasadena.

"You know what?" Peter said to his sister after she expressed how much she would miss her family. "You should come out to California with us for a few days. You're off work for now, so how about it?"

Samantha reached over at the breakfast table and patted her brother's hand. "Thanks," she said, "I might do that sometime, but not right now."

Kyle looked up from his toast and bowl of Cheerios. "You don't want to be away from your boyfriend."

Everyone stopped what they were doing and looked at Samantha.

"Who said he was my boyfriend? Besides, I'm working on a book and I have the museum to get back to after New Year's. There's a whole Christmas theme there that will need redecorating. I have the plans, but it will all take time."

Mary Elwyn looked at each of her three children and smiled. "Goodness, I feel young until I see my family together, everyone busy with their lives and fine accomplishments. We enjoy our work on the vessel, but we do miss all of you."

Dan Elwyn nodded in agreement. "That's why God made airplanes," he said with a twinkle in his blue eyes. "We need to gather together whenever we can. And, after all, we're only a cell phone call away."

As breakfast was being consumed, Samantha's cell phone rang. "Right on cue," she said as she stood and smiled, then excused herself to go into the parlor.

"Hi," she said, knowing that the caller was Gray.

"Hi, yourself," he said. "I was just sitting here at work wondering if you miss me."

Samantha sat down in her grandfather's chair and smiled. "Wow, you get paid to wonder about such things?"

"Since I'm my own boss, yes. So, do you miss me?"

"Yes," she said.

They were silent for a few moments.

"I know that your folks are leaving later today," he began. "I'm sure that means you'll want to spend as much time with them as possible. But, what about tomorrow? Might we have lunch together? I'll be in Plymouth all day. On the twenty-eighth I have an appointment in Rhode Island, but I'll be back that evening. Any thoughts for when we could get together?"

"Tomorrow sounds good," she said. "Prepare for me to be a little gloomy though. I'll have lost my parents and my brothers too. The few days they're here are wonderful, but when they leave I feel, I don't know, kind of empty."

"Oh, oh," he said. "This means I'm going to have to behave extra well; I hope I'm up for this job."

Samantha laughed. "You're cheering me up already."

"Okay, then. How about tomorrow for lunch?"

"That sounds great. Would you be interested in a picnic at your house? I make some pretty mean sandwiches and I could bring hot coffee."

"You know," he said, "I love that idea. I can make the coffee there though. Would you like me to pick you up?"

"No," she said. "I know my way. About noon?"

"Noon," he repeated. "I'll be watching the clock."

Samantha smiled and was glad that he couldn't see her blush.

Later in the day, Mary, Molly and Samantha worked together to prepare a nice meal before the trek into Boston's Logan Airport.

"I'm going to miss this," Mary said. "On the ship, we have this cook, Gus, and he's wonderful, but methodical. We can count on eating meatloaf every Tuesday, that sort of thing. And desserts, almost always it's gingerbread or apple pie. Nothing chocolate."

"Any thoughts as to how long you and Charles will carry on with this work?" Molly asked.

Mary sighed. "We've discussed it. If we retire early, in two or three years, we could afford a nice little place in either California or back here. However, if we stay with our work until we're sixty-two as we'd originally planned, we've got a number of years to go. At this point, I think Charles and I are committed to the present project and we'll just relish our time at holidays with all of you."

"We love it when you're home," Samantha said, "but we're also used to the routine, just as you are. Come home whenever you can: that's all we ask."

"There's no doubt in the world," Mary said, "your dad and I will be here whenever there's a lull in the work or a holiday. Life's too short to not make the most of it. Having all of us together may become more challenging as the three of you take on life partners. I wouldn't be at all surprised to hear that Kyle and his girlfriend will get serious and maybe married. After that, he might elect to stay in California at holidays with her and her family. Who knows?"

"Well," Molly said with a wink to Samantha, "at least we might be able to keep this one here in Plymouth." She gestured with a nod for Mary in Samantha's direction.

"Are you insinuating something, Gram?"

Molly chuckled softly. "Well, that handsome Gray seems pretty attentive. I'd love you living around the corner from me."

"That will happen anyway," Samantha said. "This is where I want to live. After Boston, which has been terrific, I'm ready for a less citified life and Plymouth is where I'll settle. It may take me a few more years to save enough for a house, but I will."

With the day passing all too fast, Samantha found herself feeling a little numb from losing her brothers and parents all at the same time. The visit had been short but, nonetheless, wonderful, and at least she had her grandparents and Lucy. And then there was Gray. She smiled thinking of her picnic lunch with him planned for the twenty-seventh.

Laying across her bed with her laptop on one side of her and Lucy on the other, Samantha planned what she would bring. What did he favor? She should have asked, she thought. Roast beef with thin slices of tomato and crispy leaves of lettuce or her chicken salad with bits of walnuts and a thin layer of cranberry sauce? She smiled deciding she would make them both. Sandwiches, chips, and something sweet.

For the remainder of that evening, Samantha worked on her book, washed her hair, then went downstairs to the parlor for a little conversation and TV watching with her grandparents.

"How many more days do we have you, Honey?" Dan Elwyn asked.

"Until after the first of the year," she said. "The museum is good until around the tenth with Christmas decorations, but after that they'll want their new theme room for the kids. It's all in motion, just a matter of getting in there to set it all up. I'll give my boss a call in a few days; she may have a specific time she'll want me in."

"What's the new theme?" Molly asked as she knitted a hat.

Samantha hugged a pillow to her middle as she sank into a deep chair. "We pretty much follow the holidays," she said. "This theme will be hearts, of course, but combined with one of my books, *Billy's Boat*, the one about the boy and his dog having sea adventures from his bedroom window. I don't know if you recall, but his boat was named the U.S.S. Valentine."

"And Billy's last name was Valentine," Molly added.

"Right," Samantha said and nodded.

"It sounds like you have a lot of fun between the museum and your books," Dan said with a smile. "Not everyone maps out as pleasant life as you have; it's very nice to see."

"It's great," Samantha said. "I mean, I'm not rich, but I manage to pay for everything I need, and I love what I do. I guess that's a sign of success."

"It certainly is," Dan said and Molly agreed.

"Tomorrow you're seeing Gray for lunch, is that right?" Molly asked.

"That's the plan," Samantha said. "I'll make sandwiches, I think. Keep it simple. We're dining at his house."

"That sounds nice. What would you like to make for sandwiches?"

"I'm going to the deli tomorrow morning; I'll buy their thin sliced roast beef; it's so good there. I'll also buy some of their roasted chicken; I thought I'd make chicken salad too. I should have asked him what he preferred."

"You can buy the roast beef because I haven't any of that left, but don't bother with the chicken; I have lots of it in the frig and you can make your good chicken salad with that. In fact, you can make up a couple of sandwiches for Gramp and me too. We love how you do those, very gourmet."

Samantha laughed. "I'd be glad to make you the sandwiches. I was going to ask you about that." Samantha stood and placed the pillow carefully back in its chair. "I think I'm going up to bed if you don't mind. I'm really tired, probably half of what I feel is just the let down from Mom, Dad, Kyle and Peter leaving. I wish they weren't so far away."

"We wish that too," Dan said. "But they'll come back when they can. Go and have a good night's sleep, Sam. You'll have a nice time tomorrow."

With smiles and hugs for each one of them, Samantha climbed the stairs to her room where she crawled into her bed, Lucy at her side. She looked at her cell phone. She could call Gray to say goodnight, but she wouldn't. She closed her eyes and slept.

The next morning when the sun invited itself into Samantha's room and across her eyes, she squinted and turned on her side facing Lucy who was meticulously cleaning her whiskers.

"Hi, Luce," she said as she reached out to stroke the cat's head. Lucy stopped her cleaning process and looked at Samantha for further instructions or compliments.

"I need coffee," she said to the cat as she moved out of bed and pulled the covers in order, disturbing Lucy just a bit. "Come on," she said to the cat as she slipped her arms into a soft robe and slid slippers onto her feet. "You can come downstairs this morning. Gram and Gramps haven't seen that much of you and I'll bet you'll get some chicken." Samantha scooped the cat up into her arms then set her down at the top of the stairway.

Entering the kitchen, Lucy beating Samantha into the room, Molly and Dan Elwyn laughed at the urgency with which the cat walked, as if the available food might disappear if she didn't hurry.

"Well," Dan began, "look who's come for breakfast. What are we having this morning, Miss Fluffy Tail? A little toast and tea?" He reached down to pat Lucy on her head.

"It's nice to see Lucy in this kitchen," Molly said. "I miss my pets. What can we get for the two of you? I have chicken for Lucy; what about you, Sweetie?" Molly stood and walked to the refrigerator. She took the covered bowl of chicken to the counter where she sliced a fair amount into a dish for Lucy who waited patiently.

Samantha smiled at the service granted to Lucy. Her grandmother had always insisted that pets be served first since they couldn't help themselves.

"I think that besides coffee, which I'm longing for, I might have one of those bananas. I'm eating lunch with Gray, so I'll keep things light this morning." Samantha poured herself a cup of coffee then sat down and reached toward the fruit bowl on the table.

Molly placed the chicken back into the refrigerator then filled a bowl with water for Lucy. "Will you leave her down now that your folks have gone back? We can keep an eye on her with the door; there's not so much coming and going now."

"I'll probably let her stay down for a while, but keeping her in my room is really okay. I know I can be paranoid about her escaping. When I go off to the deli, I'll pop her back upstairs."

"I remember," Dan said, "when she got out on us a few years ago. Remember? She was out sitting on our little potting shed roof, scared to bits."

"Yes," Samantha said with a nod. "I remember being terrified that I'd lost her. I hope that when I finally settle in a house of my own down this way, she'll be acquainted enough with her new surroundings that if she did get out, I wouldn't feel the need to panic. She's always going to be an indoor cat; I don't want to wonder where she is or if she's okay. But I'd like to think that if she escaped, she wouldn't get lost. Anyway, I think she's enjoying her visit with all of us now. She won't mind being back up in her lovely room."

"So, your picnic is going to be at Gray's house," Molly began. "I suppose that with him being an architect and all, it's a beautiful place."

Samantha swallowed a few sips of coffee. "You know, I love his house; it's nothing pretentious. It's old, not something he conjured up. He has plans for it. I think he'd like to eventually add a modern room or two, but it's just one of those charming old places like yours. It has a history, and it belongs to Plymouth."

Molly smiled. "I can picture him in a house like that, something with true character. I like that boy."

"I like him too," Samantha said and then she finished her warm brew and munched on her banana.

"So you're going off to the deli I hear," Dan Elwyn said. "Will you pick me up a few of those fantastic pickles in the barrel? Every once in a while, I need a pickle fix."

Molly laughed. "Pickles won't fix you, Dan Elwyn."

"See what I have to put up with?" he asked Samantha with a wink.

Samantha smiled and stood up, scooping Lucy into her arms. "I think this little girl has had a very nice breakfast and is ready to go back upstairs. I'll take a quick shower and then go off to pick up what I need for lunch. Are you sure I shouldn't buy some chicken, Gram?"

"Absolutely," Molly said. "I have plenty, even more for little Lucy for her supper. You can make all the chicken salad you want to, Sweetie."

With Lucy in her arms, Samantha went back upstairs, left the purring cat in her bedroom, then went for her shower. Dried and feeling refreshed, Samantha stood at her closet and thought about what to wear. She hadn't brought much with her from Boston; she'd left a variety of jeans and jerseys here and now she wished she'd brought something a little nicer. After a few moments of pushing garments aside, she came across a cobalt blue sweater and gray slacks. That would work. She brushed her long and lustrous hair then dressed in the outfit she would wear to the deli and to her lunch date with Gray. The chain bearing his carved shell was fastened in place, the perfect complement to her pretty blue sweater.

The air outside was cold but dry. It felt invigorating and she thought for a moment that she might walk to the deli rather than take her car. As she held the car keys in her right hand, Samantha made the decision to drive. Depending on what she found at the deli, it could be challenging to carry it home without it spilling.

At the deli, she chose the largest pickles she could find for her grandfather, a piece of cheesecake for each of her grandparents, two chocolate cupcakes for Gray and herself, and then the needed deli meats and bread for lunch. With three boxes and two bags to balance, Samantha was glad to have taken her car after all.

With sandwiches assembled and everything packed with care, including pretty napkins and a quart of apple cider, Samantha left her grandparents' home just before noon and pulled into Gray's driveway as he was getting out of his car.

"Hey," he said to her as she opened the car door. "I was supposed to get here first and start a nice fire."

"Does that mean we don't get a fire now?" she asked with a smile. "I brought chocolate cupcakes."

"Oh, well I guess I'll have to start the fire then. Chocolate cupcakes are so much better when you're not freezing to death."

Samantha laughed and handed him the package of sandwiches.

"Come on," he said. "I stopped by earlier and put some heat on; it won't be so bad. And once we get the hearth ablaze, it will be wonderful." Inside he struck a match and ignited the kindling beneath several tic-tac-toe arranged oak logs.

He led her into the living room and helped her out of her coat. "Do we need plates? I have a few."

"No plates," Samantha said. "I purposely brought all finger food. I have apple cider, but coffee would be nice with dessert if you have it."

"It's ready to go. I prepared the pot when I came to turn the heat up a bit; all I need to do is flip the switch. I'll go and do that. Make yourself comfortable."

Samantha looked around and then walked to the fireplace where Gray had arranged a small table and two chairs. The table was covered with a small cream-colored cloth and in the center he'd placed a little jar with a candle. Samantha sniffed at the faint scent of vanilla and then took a match from the mantle and lit the tea light just as Gray reentered the room.

"Good girl," he commented.

"I'm a candle person," she said. "I couldn't resist the vanilla scent."

Gray smiled as he placed two cups on the table for their apple cider. "The coffee's humming away in the kitchen. This picnic looks fantastic. Thank you, this was very nice of you."

"My pleasure," she said as she unbundled the sandwiches. "We have choices: roast beef and chicken salad. There are also sundried-tomato chips, a tasty but healthy alternative to the standard variety."

"I love these things," he said as he reached for one. "You thought of everything."

Samantha and Gray sat down at the small table, lifting from waxed paper diagonally sliced sandwiches onto their napkins, sprinkled with a few chips on the side.

Samantha bit into a corner of her chicken salad and looked around the room. When she had swallowed that bite, she commented on the light coming in through the windows to the North-West. "I love this room," she said.

"Me too. I can't say I'm crazy about the wallpaper though. Large cabbage roses have their place, but not here. Any suggestions?"

Samantha sipped at her apple cider. "I'm partial to colors that reflect the sea, especially in a house such as this with a view of the ocean. I could see this room in a wonderful deep blue paint or wallpaper, with soft golden lighting. Lighting is everything in a house. Overhead lights are out, except for a fixture over a dining area, but, in general, I find overhead lighting is harsh and shadowy."

Gray smiled. "I'll make a note of that. Come on," he said as he stood with part of a sandwich in his hand, "tell me what you'd do with this other front room; I guess it could be a study, or a parlor."

Samantha stood and followed him, leaving her napkin on the table. She looked around at the thick crown moldings next to the ceiling and the ornate work on the white mantle of the fireplace. "Oh," she said in a half whisper, "I'd do this room in red."

Gray laughed. "Red? So is this to reflect the Red Sea since you just got through telling me you liked the idea of using sea colors?"

Samantha gave him a quick glance. "I do love using the greens and blues of the ocean, but this room begs for warmth, for red. These wonderful old moldings all painted white, can't you envision the coziness red would bring to this space? I can imagine sitting here by the fire, reading a good book, a huge pot of tea next to me."

Gray finished the last bite of his sandwich and stood with his hands tucked into his trouser pockets. "And me, maybe?" he asked.

"And you what?" she asked.

"And me next to you, with the pot of tea, of course."

Samantha laughed. "That's a possibility. How are you at making huge pots of tea?"

Gray gestured for her to head back to their picnic in the other room. "I think I can handle it," he said. "But for now, how about some hot coffee? It should be all ready and you could undo those chocolate cupcakes you brought."

"Coffee would be perfect," she said, "and the cupcakes will be waiting for your return."

Gray gave the fire a poke then left for the kitchen where he poured two cups of black coffee. On his return to the room where Samantha sat, he asked, "Black, right? I have cream and sugar if you'd like."

"Black, thank you," Samantha said as he moved closer to sit across from her.

Gray reached for a cupcake and took about half of it in one bite. Samantha smiled watching him lose crumbs to his lap. "This thing," he said after a couple of swallows, "is dangerous. I don't think I've ever tasted such a thing. The chocolate explodes in your mouth. Thank you; these are going to be a new favorite of mine."

Samantha laughed at his eagerness. She broke her cupcake in half, enjoyed eating that small portion, then offered the other half to him.

"Are you sure?" he asked.

Samantha swallowed a few sips of coffee and shook her head yes. "I'm sure. I agree they're delicious, but the coffee is about all I can handle for now." She placed the napkin holding the remainder of the cupcake before him and watched as he devoured it in two bites. "I see you like chocolate," she said.

"Don't you?" he asked.

Samantha placed her cup down on the table. "Yes, I love it, and it loves me. It hangs right onto my hips."

"I don't blame it at all," he said with a smile. "I'd hang on to those hips too."

Samantha could feel her face grow warm and Gray smiled as he noticed it as well.

"Come on," he said. "I'll get rid of this stuff and then we can take a little walk out in the yard before I need to get back to work. Unfortunately, I have a client coming into the office around two."

Samantha stood and followed him into the kitchen and then to where he'd placed her coat. "I'd think having a client coming in would be a good thing," she said.

"Oh, don't get me wrong. I'm always glad for the clients, but I'm having a pretty nice time right here as it is. This was a great lunch, terrific food and even better company."

Samantha buttoned her coat as Gray slipped his arms into his jacket. "Let's take a look at the yard," he said. "I'd like your opinion on a couple of things. It's pretty private out to the sides and the back, which is nice. I like the contrast of having that seclusion but a front-friendly house, you know, where neighbors walk by on the sidewalk and wave to say hello as we're sitting out in our rockers on the front porch."

Samantha laughed. "In your old age, I suspect."

"And in my younger age," he said. "An hour or so in the evening to be sociable, and then out to the privacy of the back to hang out in a hammock or a nice old wicker chair."

They roamed around the yard, stopping here and there to question the variety of unknown plantings. There were little gardens formed by previous owners with piles of arranged rocks and sometimes bits of broken mortar.

"It's hard to know what this clump of dried plant is," Samantha said. She stooped down to touch its winter brittle leaves. "It almost looks like it might have been a cluster of tulips, I'm not sure. Over there," she pointed to a grouping of brown plants, "might be ferns. It's so hard to tell at this time of year. It would be a great place for ferns though; it's kind of shadowy in that spot."

Gray smiled and their eyes met. "I'm not much of a gardener, but I guess I'll learn. Maybe you could help me out in the spring; you seem to recognize some of this."

Samantha smiled. "I'm far from being an expert. I grew up knowing the plants in my grandparents' garden; that's about it. That's who you should get to help you, my grandfather. He knows what is an annual, what is a perennial, how long they last, what plant to put with another so as to have a garden in constant beauty. But, if I can help in any way, I'd enjoy that. I love growing things. In Boston, I grow cherry tomatoes on my windowsill where the sun comes flooding in. I also have a few African Violets and, of course, a Boston Fern."

"Of course," Gray said. "Well, come spring, I'll tap into Dan Elwyn's knowledge if he's willing, and I'll happily accept any help his beautiful granddaughter wishes to supply."

Gray looked briefly at his watch. "I hate to let go of this afternoon with you, but we could have another quick coffee before my appointment if you'd like."

"You go ahead to your clients. It's close to two," she said as she glanced at her own wristwatch. "We'll have other times for coffee."

Gray turned and reached out for the lapels of her coat, drawing her closer. "Like tonight?" he asked.

Samantha enjoyed a few feathery kisses and, when she thought it might develop into more, she arched back just enough to look into his wonderful eyes. "Tonight?"

"Yeah, tonight," he said pulling her closer and then firmly placing his lips on hers.

Samantha drew back enough to breathe and then pressed her forehead to his.

"Tonight," she said.

Chapter Nine

At seven-thirty that evening Samantha was with her grandmother in the kitchen washing up the last of their dinner dishes. The ringing phone interrupted their conversation about Molly's plans for painting the front hallway a lighter shade of green.

"That sounds like your cell, Sweetie. Go ahead, we'll talk later."

Samantha walked to the hallway table where she'd left her purse and picked up her cell phone. "Hi," she said with a smile on her face, knowing she had Gray on the line.

"I love hearing your voice," he said.

Samantha laughed. "You truly know all the right things to say, don't you?"

"But it's true. I love hearing your voice. So, have you had dinner yet?"

"Yes, just finished the dishes actually."

"Okay, well I'm starved. My last client just left and I thought I might grab something to devour and then have you for dessert. How's that sound?"

Samantha laughed. "I think you should definitely have dinner."

"I hear you," he said. "So, are you up for a drink someplace? It's too darn cold outside for a walk, but we could take a ride. What do you think?"

"Where are you having dinner? At home or in a restaurant?"

"Well, if I have it in a restaurant you could join me. Maybe you'd like to share an appetizer, or have a dessert and coffee. Or a glass of wine."

Samantha smiled. "Is that it? No other options?"

Gray was obviously silent for a few moments. "Okay," he finally said, "I'm going to play it very careful here and offer no further suggestions."

"Coffee while you have dinner sounds good to me. Shall I meet you someplace?"

"No. I'll leave the office now and pick you up in about ten minutes."

"Okay. Will jeans be appropriate or what?"

"Jeans," he said, "will be perfect. I'll see you in a few."

Samantha pressed her off button and closed the phone, holding it as she would his hand. She walked back into her grandmother's kitchen; Molly could tell by the smile on her granddaughter's face that it had been a call from Gray.

"Are you going out?" she asked.

"Yes. He's in need of dinner. I'll keep him company with a cup of coffee. You don't mind, do you?"

Molly wiped her wet hands on a dishtowel and moved the dried plates to a cupboard. "Of course not, Sweetie. It's good for you to get out."

"He'll be here in a few minutes, but we can talk about the hallway when I come back, or even tomorrow."

"Don't worry about the hallway," Molly said. "It's been that color for twenty years; I can certainly wait on its new color decision. I do think you're right though: a softer, brighter color would lighten the place up. I like the idea you had for a very pale green."

"We should go to the paint store tomorrow and check out the shades we like. We can bring home some samples and try them in the hallway to see what you prefer. Color makes a huge difference, but so does lighting. Gray and I were talking about lighting at his house. Overhead lighting creates shadows and can be harsh. Maybe you'd like to consider wall sconces instead of that glass piece you have there. I could see pretty lanterns in this house."

Molly smiled. "Well, you've given me a couple of really intriguing thoughts here. I love the idea of the lanterns instead of that old overhead light. Thank you, Sweetie; I think I may just want to check out lanterns tomorrow also. Now scoot, go get your coat so you'll be ready to go with that poor famished boy."

Samantha laughed. "Okay, we'll talk later, Gram." She poked her head into the living room to say goodbye to her grandfather then went to answer the door where she found the handsome John Eldon Grayson.

"Hi there," he said with a smile. "Should I say hello to your grandparents before I steal you away?"

"I think they'll understand if you don't. They know we're heading out so that you can have some dinner. I'm all set if you are," she said while slipping her arms into her coat.

They walked to Gray's warm car and drove just minutes away to a local restaurant known for its seafood.

"This okay with you?" he asked as they parked.

"Sure. I haven't been here for years. Did they change the name? Bluewater Grill is not something I recall."

"Yeah, this place has changed owners a couple of times in the past ten years or so. It's been the Bluewater Grill for a few years though, and the seafood chef knows what he's doing. They also have a little live music here most evenings. It's casual but nice."

"Sounds good," she said as they stepped out of the car and walked toward the restaurant door.

Once seated and their order taken, Samantha folded her linen napkin across her lap and asked, "So, was this client you were with today someone local?"

"Not Plymouth, the Wareham area. I've had this client for several years. I actually designed both his home in Hyannis and his son's home in Harwich. They're nice people, easy to work with."

Samantha nodded. "That makes it so much more pleasant."

"How's your job at the museum? Do you work pretty independently?"

"Yes, but I still have to answer to Julie. She's a friend but also the director, so everything needs to pass her approval. Most of the time she's okay with what I have planned, but there are those times, you know, where there's a difference of opinion."

"So, you wouldn't be sad to leave there?"

Samantha smiled. "I have no immediate plans to leave, but no, I'd be fine with moving on. I love the room planning; I've had a lot of fun with that, but I have a bazillion ideas. I'll always find something to do that I love."

Gray's meal of baked scallops was served and Samantha's black coffee was placed before her.

"This looks good," Gray commented. "Would you care to share?"

"No, thank you. It does look good though. So, when will you begin this project for these people, and what is it?"

Gray swallowed a bite of his dinner then said, "They're working on building a five-store unit, something very classy, steeples, gables, the works. The son has a chain of shops on the Cape; he's opening a new place in this unit, and another family member wants to open a French café. I'm thinking I'll have fun with this one, except for square footage in each place, they've given me free reign."

Samantha sipped her hot coffee. "Wow. We're really fortunate, aren't we? How many people have work they truly enjoy?"

"Absolutely," he said. "And I also have a house in Plymouth I'm working on for another client, an antique, with three rooms to be added in keeping with the Colonial aspect but will incorporate the modern conveniences. That's fun too, and I'll learn as I go what to do with my own place. I know I'll want to add a room or two, but I've been a little slow at getting down exactly what I want to accomplish. Maybe you could help me out with that aspect."

Samantha laughed. "You might be sorry. I can be enormously evil when it comes to design. I come up with some complicated ideas. The work crew at the museum gives me a hard time about what I request to be built. In the end though, they like the results."

Gray continued with his meal then took a swallow of water.

"I like unique ideas," he said. "If you're willing to work on the design with me, I'll be glad for the suggestions."

"I think that would be fun," she said. "And, if I make a suggestion you don't care for, I won't be offended. It's your house, after all, and you're the one who needs to find it satisfying."

Gray sat back in his chair and smiled at her. "I appreciate that. So, what are you up to tomorrow? I have the day in Rhode Island. I should be back in Plymouth by five or six. Would you be available for dinner?"

"That sounds nice," she said.

"Where would you like to go? Do you have a favorite place here in town, or anywhere for that matter? We can do whatever you wish."

Samantha thought for a moment then said, "How about The Salty Dog? Their menu looks appealing, like comfort food. I noticed they have stuffed peppers and macaroni and cheese. Do you like that kind of fare?"

"Oh, yeah, love it. There should be music there tomorrow night too. I'm glad you thought of going there."

Samantha sat back, relaxed and enjoying the feel of the warm coffee cup in her hands.

Gray looked at her, dabbed his mouth with his napkin and sat back as well. "Do you get the feeling that we're old souls? I mean, it really feels like we've known each other a long time."

"Do you mean as in another life?" she asked with a faint smile.

Gray looked at her and appraised her beautiful face. "Maybe."

"Do you believe in that sort of thing?"

"Am I in trouble if I do? Actually, I don't know. It's hard to believe in something intangible, but I'm no expert on the subject. I guess I'd say I'm open to possibilities."

Samantha straightened up and placed her empty cup on its saucer. "I would have to agree with you. I'm not sure what I think about the old soul or reincarnation theories. But we do seem to have a sense of comfort in being together. It's nice."

After deciding they wouldn't have anything else there, the bill was delivered to Gray and paid for. Together they stood, slipped their arms into their coats and left the restaurant for the car.

"Where to?" Gray asked. "It's a little after nine. Would you like to go someplace else for a drink or something?"

"The coffee was just what I needed," she said. "And since you have an early day going off to Rhode Island tomorrow, maybe we should just plan on seeing one another tomorrow evening for dinner."

"Oh, not so fast," he said with a smile as he maneuvered the car out onto the main road and toward the harbor. "Unless you're too tired, how about if we just sit by the water, watch the boats with their lights bobbing around?"

"That's fine with me," she said.

Within moments they pulled head-in to the harbor's view; Gray left the engine on for warmth as he put the car in park.

"I never get tired of this scenery," Samantha said. "Even in the dark, it's a very beautiful place."

"It is," Gray said. "I love it here, but I also think about the rough life some of these people lead on the sea. That wouldn't be for me at all. I like the tour boats; we stay within sight of land, but fishing wouldn't appeal at all."

Samantha was quiet and rested her head back against the seat of the warm car, her eyes fastened on a boat where three golden lights seemed to move in a perfect rhythm.

Gray looked at her, light reflecting on her face from an overhead street lamp. She was beautiful, but not the kind of girl who was aware of it. She turned to look at him, feeling his stare.

"What?" she said.

"Just enjoying the scenery," he said with a smile. "And thinking...."

"Thinking what?"

"You remind me so much of something, can't figure out what it is."

Samantha was quiet for a moment and then she reached over and lightly punched his right arm as he laughed.

"If you even mention once about my mother's hamster, I will get out of this car and become only a memory, I swear I will."

Gray laughed again. "Are you sure you don't want a nightcap? A glass of wine someplace?"

"Not really. Do you?"

"No, I'm good."

Samantha looked at the clock on his dashboard. "It's ten o'clock. Wouldn't you like to get to bed?"

"Is that an invitation?" he asked with a twinkle in his eyes.

"No, it is not. But Rhode Island calls."

"You're right. You're a nag about the time, but you're right." He smiled as he put the car in reverse, backed up into the street then drove toward the Elwyn house just minutes away.

In front of the driveway, Samantha reached for her door handle as he stopped. "Don't get out," she said. "I'll scoot along and let you get some rest."

Gray put the car in park and moved to walk toward Samantha's side. "A gentleman never lets a lady walk away from him like that," he said.

Samantha smiled and allowed him to assist her then felt the warmth of his hand securing hers as they walked to the side door of the house. They hesitated, looked at one another, and then he placed both of his large hands on the sides of her face drawing her to him in a light, then long kiss.

When they released one another, Gray looked at her and said, "Tomorrow evening."

"Tomorrow evening," she repeated softly.

Inside her grandparents' home, Samantha hung her coat in the hallway closet and then tiptoed toward the living room in case they were asleep. She found her grandmother crocheting while watching TV and her grandfather, his head down and off to one side, snoring softly.

"Hi," she said in a whisper to her grandmother.

Molly Elwyn smiled and put her crocheting down on her lap. "Hello, Sweetie. How was your evening?"

Samantha sat down across from her grandmother. "It was very nice. I had coffee while Gray had dinner at The Bluewater Grill. It used to be Payson's, remember?"

Molly nodded her head. "Yes, it was Payson's, then it was something else for a couple of years. I wonder if they keep the same chef, it's said to be consistently good. We haven't been there since it was Payson's though. Your grandfather and I don't eat out that much. The man likes home cooking." Molly smiled and looked in his direction.

Samantha glanced over at her grandfather, his mouth parted just a bit as he slept.

"You two have a nice life here. You're my examples."

Molly laughed. "Oh dear, don't expect much excitement then. I would agree with you, we have a nice life, I wouldn't want it anywhere else or anyway else. My favorite place in the whole world is right here in this chair, in this room, with my family. I guess it doesn't get much better than that."

Samantha smiled. "That's it. That's what I hope for."

"You'll get it, Sweetie. Now, what's up for tomorrow? Are we going off to look at lanterns and paint for the hallway?"

"Yes," Samantha said. "I think we should. How about Gramps? Will he want some input?"

Molly threw her head back and laughed. "No and, if he did, we'd ignore it anyway. He has terrible taste in colors. Have you noticed the combination of shirt colors and socks? It's disgraceful! No, we'll choose the paint and lanterns. He'll love whatever we select."

Samantha stood. "Okay," she said with a smile as she leaned forward and planted a light kiss on her grandmother's cheek. "I'm going up. I'll have a little visit with Lucy and then some delicious sleep. Tomorrow will be fun. We should plan to have tea or coffee out together, just as a little treat."

Molly smiled. "I like that idea. Never had a daughter to do those things with, so I'll enjoy that. Have a good night's rest, Dear."

When morning arrived, Samantha found Lucy meticulously cleaning her paws and whiskers about two inches from Samantha's face. She squinted against the sun and then moved back a few inches away from the cat who looked at her as if questioning the value of increased distance.

"Hi, Luce," she said as she reached out and gave the cat a few head and neck pats. Samantha swung her legs out of bed on the other side and headed to the washroom, then back into the bedroom where she made the bed around Lucy who looked as if she'd grumble if she could. "Come on, Luce, cooperate just a little here, would you?" When the bed was neatly made, Samantha took Lucy's water bowl to the washroom, rinsed it out and filled it with cold water. She placed it down on a mat then filled her food bowl with a small can of cat food and a bit of kibble. "There," she said to the inquisitive, cat. "Your Majesty has breakfast. Now be good. I'm getting dressed and leaving for a while. I'll see you later today. I promise."

With coffee, eggs and toast under their belts, Molly and Samantha headed for downtown in Samantha's car. They decided to stop at the local hardware store for paint, then on to a place where they could search for the lanterns. After more than an hour looking at paint chips in varying shades of green-gray, and selecting a flat finish to soften the walls, Samantha suggested they try one of the large home improvement stores for the lanterns. Once there, the choices were unending and Molly was delighted with her final decision, oblong copper lanterns and a dimmer switch so that they could be kept very low for most of the time and turned up higher when needed.

"I feel like a kid at Christmas," she said to Samantha as they drove to a small coffee shop in the center of town. "I can't wait to see those lanterns up. I'll paint the walls first, then your grandfather can put them up. Thank goodness he's handy like that. The man can do most anything."

Samantha smiled. "I agree. He's multi-talented. And I'll help paint the hallway with you later today. I actually love doing things like that."

They pulled up, parallel parking almost in front of the café in Plymouth's historic center. "How about this?" Samantha asked. "They saved us a space."

Molly laughed. "It seems so. This is such fun, Sweetie. I haven't been in a home improvement store in years, and now I have these wonderful lanterns and that lovely soft color we chose for the hall. Then to top it off, tea with my granddaughter. This is so nice."

Samantha put the car in park and turned off the engine. They both reached for their doors and walked inside the café where they sat at a window's round table and ordered scones and tea. The view from where they sat was like looking at a postcard. The historic buildings were wonderful, and just the way the sun was gleaming on the bricks and ornate mortar to the corners of the structures, it could easily have been a painter's rendition of the wonderful old town.

Samantha thought the only thing that could have added perfection would have been the presence of Gray. She smiled and Molly caught the moment.

Looking at her granddaughter, Molly said, "You have Gray on your mind."

Samantha laughed. "Just a tad. I was thinking about how he must love the architecture here in town. He seems to love the mix of old and new."

"As do I," Molly said. "I've lived here all of my life and never once wished I could live anywhere else. This town has it all: beauty, convenience, everything."

"And that's why I want to live here too," Samantha said. "If there's any place at all I would have called home as a kid, it was here, coming to visit you and Grampa. I'll be totally out of sorts when I need to go back to Boston. Not that it isn't great there, it is. I love that old city. But, it isn't home, plain and simple."

As Molly and Samantha stood and prepared to leave the café, Samantha turned and almost collided with a young woman she instantly knew she'd seen before. It was Karry, the young woman she'd seen dancing with Gray at Pilgrim's Place Pub on the night of his birthday.

As she began to apologize, she noticed the carved shell, so similar to her own, on a chain around the blonde's neck. Her eyes were fastened to it, and then Karry noticed that Samantha was wearing hers as well.

"Oh," she began, "aren't these the best things? Gray is so talented, isn't he?" She flashed a set of the whitest teeth Samantha had ever seen.

"Yes," she answered and then she moved, anxious to get out of that place, her thoughts going to Gray who had said that only one other person, other than his mother, had one of those shells he'd carved. And that one other person was an elderly woman. What was this about? There was no doubt at all that Karry's necklace was the same work. Had he neglected to tell her about a fourth shell? It troubled her and she was unusually quiet once they climbed back into her car.

"Are you okay?" Molly asked. "You seem to have shut down after bumping into that young woman. Did she say something offensive?"

Samantha put the key in the ignition and started the car. She backed up a few feet, then, shifting into drive, she moved forward and carefully maneuvered the automobile out into the street and toward home. "No, she didn't say anything negative; I just don't care for her much."

Molly stole a side glance at Samantha's pretty profile. If she wanted to discuss it, she would. Otherwise, Molly would leave the subject alone.

Now Samantha wasn't so sure about the evening planned with Gray. She didn't relish thinking about asking him to explain Karry's shell, and she didn't like the idea of letting it go. After a few hours of hallway painting with her grandmother, she spent time in her bedroom with Lucy, reading and going over her latest book. She decided to tell Gray she wasn't feeling up to going out. She could not, would not, be with him for dinner. At that point, she didn't want to see him ever again.

Chapter Ten

Samantha slept restlessly that night. She'd lied to Gray about feeling ill, and now she felt genuinely sick. She wanted to accuse him of telling her an untruth and she wanted him to have a good explanation, but this was Karry, the flirtatious, physically tempting blonde with an apparent ability to cause pain and envy. Why, she wondered, did she allow this kind of incident to happen and affect her so profoundly? Samantha knew that her own insecurities were part of the problem, and yet she had no idea what to do about it. Her worst fears, that she was not enough for Gray, confronted her and caused her to decide to run.

"I wish you didn't have to go," Molly Elwyn said to Samantha as she watched her granddaughter pack a few things to go back to Boston. "I thought we'd have you for another week or so. I'll really miss you and Lucy."

"I'll miss you too," Samantha said as she scooped the cat up and into her pet carrier. "I'll call you when I get back to my place. I think I'll leave Lucy off and let her get settled in, then I'll pop over to the museum. If I can get that room redecorated by the end of the week, Julie will be happy and I'll have it off my mind."

"Could I carry something downstairs for you, Sweetie? You travel so light."

"I'm fine, Gram. I just have this little overnight bag and Lucy. I'll leave the rest of my clothes here; I'll be back again before you know it."

At the bottom of the stairs Dan Elwyn greeted his wife and granddaughter with a frown. "I wish you could stay longer," he said.

Samantha put the pet carrier down and hugged her grandparents. "I know, but I'll be back; you can't get rid of me. The timing is just, well, I think this is best."

Dan looked at Molly and they said nothing, though each had their feelings that it was an issue of some sort involving the heart and Gray.

Driving with the morning traffic was not something that Samantha was used to and she was amazed at the slow pace, the stops and goes. Feeling incredibly lonely and empty inside, she maneuvered the car carefully through the expressway congestion and then on the narrow streets of Boston. At her apartment, she let Lucy out of the carrier first, then changed her clothes and made a cup of tea.

With the museum in her thoughts, she was glad to have that topic take up space in her mind to crowd out thoughts of Gray. She left food and water for the perplexed cat and then grabbed a knee length coat. She locked her door, forgot to drink even a sip of her tea, then made her way over to the museum.

In record time, she took decorations down and packed them away, then stopped in to visit Julie in her office. "I have the Valentine project all planned," she said. "I was thinking I'd get that going over the next few days if that's okay with you. I know I'm a bit early, but while the museum is closed today and tomorrow, I thought it might be a good time to begin."

Julie sat back in her chair and sighed. "I hope we can do exactly that, Sam, but we may have an issue."

"What's that?" Samantha asked.

Julie stood and walked around her desk, placing folders in a file cabinet. She turned and looked at Samantha. "We have a leak in the roof. Ice managed to sneak beneath the eaves and it's caused some damage. The construction crew is coming in later today to estimate the situation but, if it's bad, it may mean closing the museum until the work is done. I hate to, but it would be too risky to have people, especially kids, wandering around with ladders and maybe even ceilings being taken down and put up."

"It's that bad?" Samantha asked.

Julie nodded. "I'm afraid so. We won't actually know until they get in there and see the extent of the ice damage, but it could mean that we'll be out of the picture for a while."

"The ice went under the eaves?"

"Under the eaves and through the roof. Two possible problems. I'm hoping for a quick solution, but this is an ancient building; we have no idea what we're facing. I can give you a call tomorrow after the inspection. By then, I'll have a good idea if we'll need to close our doors for a period of time. I really hate this."

"Me too," Samantha said as she sank into a plush chair.

Back at her apartment, Samantha found her cold tea and placed it in the microwave to heat it. She stood at her kitchen window, waiting for the tea, when her eyes traveled the cityscape which Gray had commented on during a visit. As great as the view was, her heart was in Plymouth for more reasons than one.

With her hot tea she moved to the living room and sat down next to the phone. She dialed her grandparents' number and felt a sense of longing when she heard Molly's voice.

"Hi, Gram, just checking in. I went off to the museum for a while, took down the Christmas decorations in the children's area, and got hit with the news that the museum might have to close for a time. They have leaks due to ice."

"Oh, that's a shame," Molly said. "It's such a lovely old building, but who knows what they did to secure them years ago? I suppose this could mean a major overhaul."

"Yes, it could, but I'm hoping not. However it will give me time to work on my new book. How are you and Gramp?"

"We miss you. And you know if the museum is closing for a bit, you could come back here and work on that book. We'd love that you know."

Samantha smiled and reached out to pat Lucy. "I know. I'll have to wait and see how things go. Julie is going to call me tomorrow; they won't know what the extent of the damage is until then. It's really a mess. I'm just hoping for a *small* mess."

"So, what are you doing now, Sweetie? And our little Lucy, how's she doing?"

"Lucy is fine; she's right here with me. And me, well, I'm bummed out about the museum, but I have hot tea and that's always a plus. I'll find out what's going on tomorrow and I'll give you a call, Gram. Say hi to Gramps for me, and love to you both from Lucy and me."

They said their goodbyes and Samantha leaned back against the soft cushions of the sofa. Her apartment was nice; she felt fortunate to have such a great place, but it seemed stark compared to her grandparents' home. She looked around and wondered about what she might do to bring warmth to this space.

Leaving her tea to cool and Lucy asleep on the sofa, Samantha stood and walked to her bedroom closet where she kept a box of family photos. One by one she went through them, finding a nice picture of her parents on the day they were married, and high school pictures of both of them. She found pictures of Molly and Dan when they were years younger, and photos of her brothers and herself when they were children.

Samantha took the box into the living room and sipped at her warm tea. She selected more than a dozen pictures she decided to frame and hang on the wall across from her sofa. She would buy frames, and that became her project over the next twenty-four hours.

The next day, with pictures framed and hung as symmetrical as she could manage the varying sizes, the phone rang and she answered it to hear Julie's voice.

"Not good news, Sam. We're in for major renovations. The inspection led from one thing to another, so the trustees have decided to get everything done and over with all at once. We're going to be closed for at least a month. The publicity information is going out today with regrets. So find yourself a place in the sun someplace. We're down and out for a while."

When Samantha finished speaking with Julie, she placed the phone back on its receiver and groaned. Within moments, the phone rang again and, expecting it to be Julie telling her something she'd forgotten to mention, Samantha picked it right up without checking to see who the caller was.

"Hi," he said. "Feeling any better?"

His voice seemed subdued to Samantha. "Yeah, I'm okay."

"Sam," he said after a few moments, "I stopped by your grandparents' house an hour ago to bring them a plant that wasn't doing well in my office. They said nothing of you being sick. Now I'm wondering. What happened?"

Samantha sighed and closed her eyes for a moment. Then she looked across the room at the framed pictures of her family and even a snapshot of Lucy.

"Sam? You there?"

"Yes," she said, "I'm here."

"What happened? We were doing great I thought. Did I have that wrong?"

Samantha felt tears form in her eyes. "I thought we were

doing great too. I think maybe we were just moving things along too fast. I don't know."

Gray could be heard taking a deep breath. "Look, Sam, if I scared you away, let me prove to you that I can slow down. If it was up to me, I'd be hanging out with you twenty-four, seven. I get that that might be a little overwhelming. But I've held back; I was trying to take it easy with you. What can I do to make things better?"

Samantha looked around the room and brought her eyes back to the pictures. "I don't know, Gray. I just need some time. Please, let me have some time."

He was quiet and then he said, "Okay. You know where I am. I'm not going anywhere with anyone, Sam. I'll hope for your call."

Samantha hesitated then placed the phone down, tears streaming from her beautiful green eyes. Lucy brushed up against her as if consoling her friend.

After three more days of working on her book and taking brief walks near to her apartment, Samantha decided it was time to get out of there for a while. She thought about going to Chicago to visit Will, or to California to see her brothers, but then she would need someone to take care of Lucy. The idea of going to Plymouth made her feel a wave of nausea, but she finally decided that she would go there where she was loved and she would stay in the house, out of sight. She called her grandparents, asked them not to say anything about her return to Gray if they saw him, and then prepared clothing and Lucy's needs to head back to the South Shore and beautiful Plymouth.

Once she and Lucy were settled back into her grandparents' home, Samantha began to feel the comfort surrounding her. Two wonderful people to live and interact with, and the familiarity and warmth of the old house, gave Samantha the courage and interest to get back to work on her book. She would also consider other options to keep her busy over the next few weeks. She found herself going out for walks very early in the morning or after dinner when it was dark. She needed to breathe in the fresh sea air and to spend the energy with the exercise, but she didn't want to run into Gray or his family. She needed this alone time, still feeling injured from seeing the beautiful shell on a chain around Karry's neck. Her own shell was placed carefully away in a small jewelry box she'd had as a child at her grandparents' home. She loved the shell. She would never let anything happen to it, but wearing it now was like wearing a hot coal. She just couldn't stand to be reminded of who else had something so precious from Gray.

While sipping hot coffee and eating a slice of toast for breakfast a week after she'd arrived back in Plymouth, Dan Elwyn walked into the kitchen and sat down across from Samantha and Molly. "Saw Gray a few minutes ago at the news stand," he said.

Samantha looked at her grandfather and then at Molly.

Dan Elwyn looked at his granddaughter and then at his wife. "I guess it's not any of my business."

Samantha placed her coffee cup down on its saucer and looked at him. "It is, of course it is, Gramps. I've been rude not mentioning it to either of you. I'm just a little upset about something. I'm not shutting you out; I haven't wanted to talk about it, that's all."

"You don't have to tell us a thing, Sweetie," her grandmother said. "It is your business. We're here if you want to talk, but if you don't, that's okay," she said as she gave her husband a stern look.

Samantha moved her plate and partially eaten toast away and folded her hands on the table. "It's the shell he gave me."

When neither of her grandparents spoke but looked confused, she continued.

"Gray gave that to me and I was elated. It's the most beautiful and personal thing anyone has ever given me. I love it. But he told me that only two other people had one, his mother and an elderly woman who requested one. The day we had tea and scones in that café in town, Gram, and I bumped into that girl, she had one she was wearing."

Molly looked surprised but said nothing.

"Maybe there's a reason she had it," Dan Elwyn offered. "Maybe Gray didn't make that one."

"No," Samantha said, "it was Gray's work, I'm positive. And what explanation could he have, Gramps? I hate it that he may have lied to me. I cannot stand lies. How do you ever know when to believe someone if they lie to you? They can swear they're telling the truth, and maybe they are, but once they lie, the trust is shaken."

Molly and Dan looked at one another.

"Sweetie," her grandmother said, "I don't have a reason for this happening. All I know is that to have hurt you this much, you must really love Gray. And I'm pretty good about observing others. I'd say he is definitely crazy about you. Do you think you could talk to him about it? Wouldn't it be fair to give him the chance to explain?"

Samantha looked away and didn't know what to reply.

"It was a bit awkward this morning seeing him," Dan said. "He was as polite as always when we saw one another, but he didn't even mention your name. I knew right off that he was troubled about your relationship. You can see it in his eyes."

Samantha stood and took her cup, saucer and plate to the sink. "I don't want to put you two in a difficult situation," she said. "Maybe it would be best if I went back into Boston."

"No," Molly began, "it wouldn't. You stay right here. You're not putting us in any situation at all. When family members have injuries, we take care of one another. We love you and we want you here. What you do about Gray is entirely up to you. Right Dan?"

"Of course it is," he said. "We're behind you whatever you decide."

"Thank you," she said as she turned from the sink to face them. "But don't feel that you need to avoid him or to tell him anything untrue about my whereabouts. If he discovers I'm here and he calls, I can handle it. I'll be fine. I think I'll go back upstairs if you don't mind. I'm slow at this book; I think I'm going to rewrite a few sections."

"That's fine, Sweetie," Molly said. "Come down when you feel like it. I have some nice corn chowder for lunch, but I can heat you a bowl whenever you're ready."

Samantha leaned over and placed kisses on her grandparents' cheeks, then turned and went back upstairs to her work and to the napping Lucy.

The next few days were uneventful. Samantha called Will in Chicago and her brothers in California to tell them about the museum's misfortune and that she could be reached in Plymouth.

On one evening when it was not too cold, Samantha decided to go out for a walk. "I won't go far and I won't be long," she said, "but if either or both of you want to come along for the fresh air, I'd enjoy your company."

"You know what," Dan Elwyn began, "I'll go. I haven't been out for a walk in ages. We're so dependent on our vehicles to get us around, I'm not sure these old feet recall taking one step after another. What about it, Molly, my Sweet? Want to come?"

Molly laughed. "I should, there's no doubt about it, but I'll stay here. When the weather is a bit more spring-like, I'll venture out. When you come home, I'll have a brand new pot of coffee made and if that doesn't interest you we can warm up some cider."

"With a touch of brandy added for color," Dan said with a twinkle in his blue eyes.

"Come on, Gramp," Samantha urged. "Let's grab our coats and gloves. We won't be long, Gram. I'll have that coffee when we get back."

They walked out and downhill toward the harbor. From there, they began to walk to the right, south of the town's center. It was dark enough that most homes had lights on inside and Samantha loved looking at the houses, aglow with warmth.

"Did you ever wonder what they're doing inside?" Dan asked his granddaughter as he caught her gaze toward the well-lit homes.

Samantha smiled. "You read my mind. Yes, I always wonder. I imagine them in there baking chocolate chip cookies and drinking home brewed beer."

"Now that's a combination," Dan said with a grin. "I love seeing the lights and the colors people choose to live with. Even through the curtains, you can make out wall colors. Does that make me weird, that I notice that stuff?"

Samantha laughed. "Well, Gramp, if you're weird, so am I. I love to see how other people live. And I don't feel nosey, just interested. Sometimes I look at houses and think that maybe there are people in there I'd really like to know."

No sooner had she said the words, she looked up to find herself in front of Gray's house. His car was there and the lights were on.

Dan Elwyn noticed that Samantha was standing still with her eyes fixed on this antique home. "What is it, Sam? Did you see something?"

Samantha shivered and turned her eyes from the house to

her grandfather. "This is Gray's home," she said. And when she looked back at the lit windows, she could see movement inside, and then the walls in the front room on the left being painted red as she'd suggested.

Dan noticed her eyes glimmering with moisture. "Are you okay? Would you like to knock on the door and say hello, or would you prefer to get the heck out of here?"

Samantha smiled at her grandfather, always sensitive and so dear in his consideration of another's thoughts. "I'm okay. I guess I'm just surprised to find myself here. We've taken a good walk for ourselves; let's go home and have some of Gram's hot coffee."

"Sounds good," he said, then he looked back at Gray's house as they turned and walked toward home. "Nice house he has there. I'm not terribly surprised though, he always won the history debates, knew his stuff when it came to local events and dates too. Bet he knows the ins and outs of that place."

Samantha stuck her hands further into her pockets and was glad to be heading back. "He does," she said. "It's important to him to keep the integrity of that house with the new renovations. It will be beautiful, I'm sure."

Dan Elwyn knew it would be best not to pursue the subject of Gray and his house unless Samantha did. She said nothing else as they walked briskly back toward town and the comfortable old home just three hundred yards from the harbor.

"Boy," Dan said as they approached the side door, "I sure could use a nice hot cup of something. Bet you could too, Honey."

"I'd love something warm," she said. "The walk was invigorating though, don't you think?"

Dan laughed as they entered the kitchen and he hung their coats and scarves in the entryway closet. "It was invigorating all right. I think my right knee is going to be happy to stretch out in the recliner though."

Samantha smiled. "Go and sit down, Gramp. Is it cider you prefer? I'll bring it to you."

"Who's bringing what where?" Molly asked as she entered the kitchen with a smile.

"The old knee is complaining," Dan said. "My darling granddaughter has offered to deliver some warmed cider to me in my chair."

Molly smiled at Samantha. "What a good girl," she said. "How about you, Sweetie? What will you have?"

Samantha thought for a moment then said she'd have some hot coffee.

"I'll get it for you; you take the cider to your poor old grandfather, then I'll tell you about your phone call."

Samantha looked at her grandmother then walked to the living room where Dan sat with his legs propped up on the recliner's foot rest. "Here you are, Gramp," she said. "Is there anything else I can get for you?"

"No, thank you, Dear. This is perfect."

Samantha returned to the kitchen where her grandmother poured steaming coffee into a rose decorated mug. "So what's this about a call? Was it Julie with information about the museum?"

Molly poured herself a cup of coffee and sat down at the kitchen table, inviting Samantha to do the same. "No," she said, "it was Gray."

Samantha's heart felt as if it had done hop-scotch. "Gray called?"

"Yes, he did," Molly said with a direct look into her granddaughter's beautiful eyes.

"What did he want? What did he say?"

Molly smiled. "He said he had been painting his front room and that he had your lovely face flash into his thoughts. He felt a strong urge to connect with you."

Samantha shook her head. "That's really strange. Gramps and I were walking and I suddenly realized we were there, in front of his house. I could see him inside painting."

Molly's smile faded. "Now that's a connection," she said. "To think that you were outside of his place, you see him in there working, and he thinks of you. That's telepathy. You two have something important going on."

Samantha swallowed a sip of her coffee then stared into the dark brew for just a moment before looking up into her grandmother's face. "Does he know I'm here?"

"Yes," Molly said. "He asked me if I knew where you were. Apparently he's called your number in Boston. He said he'd left a message. He wanted to know if I knew your whereabouts. I didn't want to lie to him, Sweetie."

"No, it's okay, Gram. I wouldn't want you to be put in that

position of telling him anything but the truth." She thought about him having left a message in Boston. Gray hated leaving messages, yet he had.

"He'd love you to call him," Molly said.

Samantha looked into her grandmother's blue eyes. "Did he say that?"

Molly smiled. "His voice said that. He sounded so genuine, Sam. The boy cares about you. I don't know what happened with the shell that girl had, but I don't see Gray as being the type who would tell you something if it wasn't the truth."

Samantha finished her coffee then stood and took her mug to the sink. "I think I'll go upstairs, Gram. The walk was great, but a warm bath and a good book with Lucy is about all I'm up for right now." She moved to kiss her grandmother goodnight before going into the living room to say goodnight to her grandfather.

After her bath and getting into a pair of pajamas, Samantha slid under the covers of her bed and invited Lucy to join her. The cat licked her whiskers and cleaned her paws, then leaped onto the bed nearly knocking her book out of Samantha's hands.

"Thanks," she said to the cat as she ruffled her ears and neck. "You could be just a little more lady-like, you know."

The next day Samantha took the last can of food for Lucy from her closet and made a mental note to pick up some more. "Maybe I'll even buy you a can of people tuna," she told the cat, whose eyes grew wide in what appeared to be joyful anticipation."

Over breakfast with her grandparents, Samantha drank tea and munched cinnamon toast as she told them that she was planning a trip to McHenry's for cat food, asking if they needed anything else from the shop.

"Oh, would you mind picking up the newspaper, Honey?" Dan Elwyn asked. "I'll take it easy on the old knee today."

Molly smiled at her husband and granddaughter.

"I'd be glad to pick it up for you, Gramps. I'll get changed and leave in a few minutes."

Up in her room, Samantha chose to wear jeans and a navy blue jersey. She looked at the shell she'd left in her old jewelry box, then turned and slipped socks and shoes onto her slim feet. She longed to see Gray, she yearned to wear the shell his fingers had carved, but she wouldn't, not yet.

Downstairs in the front hallway, she slipped her arms into a mid-thigh length red jacket and called out that she was leaving. The walk to McHenry's wasn't more than a ten minute trek and she would enjoy the crisp morning air. Inside the small store, she picked up a newspaper and tucked it under her left arm before she went to the aisle for cat food. She selected ten cans with a good variety and the promised can of people tuna then headed for the cash register with her arms full. As she stood in line, two cans of cat food dropped and rolled. As she reached for them, a large hand retrieved them and, as they both stood, she realized she was looking directly into Gray's face.

"Did you have a yen for a little fish?" he asked with a devilish smile as he handed the cans to her, each marked Tasty Salmon Morsels.

Samantha felt stunned but then she replied, "Very funny."

With a more serious face he asked, "Do you have time for a cup of coffee with me?"

Samantha felt tongue-tied as she looked down at the counter where she placed the tins of food and the newspaper. "I promised my grandfather I'd get the paper for him. He likes to read it in the morning."

"We can drop it off to him," Gray pleaded.

Samantha took a deep breath. "I guess that would be okay."

She paid for her purchases, Gray paid for his newspaper and a package of mints, then they walked out to his car together and headed for the Elwyn home.

Within minutes, Samantha and Gray were sitting in the coffee shop across from one another, steaming mugs of black coffee before them.

"What's happened to us, Sam? I need to know. I haven't been able to think of anything else. I question every move I made. I go to sleep with you on my mind and I wake up the same way. What's going on?"

Samantha looked away and then back into his wonderful amber eyes. "The shell," she said, "the one you carved for me at Christmas. You told me there were only three."

"That's true," he said.

Samantha looked away again and then into her black coffee before she met his eyes. "I saw someone else with one," she said.

"That's not possible. Who? Do you know the person?"

"Karry," Samantha said, determined to be direct.

"Karry?" he said incredulously. "What the heck?" He shook his head. "The woman I made the other shell for was Mrs. Demitri. She was in her eighties when she died last year. I'd bet that Karry's grandmother was given that shell and it ended up with Karry. The two women were friends. That's my only explanation, Sam. Karry would not be someone for whom I'd carve a shell. She just isn't."

Samantha looked away for a moment then back at his handsome face. "I hate it that she has it."

"Me too," he said. "But if you get a chance to take a close look sometime, you'll see the name Alexis carved in the waves, just the way I carved Samantha into yours. You won't find Karry on that shell anywhere. I promise you that."

Samantha rubbed her eyes then took a sip of her coffee.

"Is that all?" he asked. "Is there anything else? Because if there isn't, I want us back on, just the way we were. Your grandmother told me about the museum."

Samantha nodded. "Yes, it's a mess. What time was it when you phoned my grandparents' home last night?"

Gray thought for a moment then said, "Around seven-thirty, I think. Why?"

"I was walking with my grandfather and at just about that time, I found myself standing before your house. I could see you painting the walls red."

Gray smiled. "So, you know that I took the advice of someone special."

Samantha smiled.

"And you know that although I've been thinking of you every moment, the very fact that you were outside my door must have been what drove me to call your grandparents. I tried calling in Boston a few times."

Samantha smiled. "I know, Gram told me that you'd even left a message."

Gray shook his head and smiled. "Yeah. And you know I hate doing that. I just couldn't wait any longer. I know I left it that I'd leave the ball in your court but, Sam, you don't play ball well."

Samantha looked toward the window and the bay.

"Any chance that I'm forgiven?" he asked.

Samantha drew her eyes away from the sea and back to

Gray. "Maybe."

"I'll take that as a yes," he said.

Samantha took several sips of her coffee but said nothing in response.

"Sam? Am I wrong to think we're on track again?"

Samantha loosened the scarf around her neck and shifted in her seat. "I miss what we had," she said. "I know myself and I understand very well that I can be slow to heal. Even though you gave me a good reason for Karry to be wearing that shell, it just irks me to the point that it's as if I'm now a cracked plate and afraid to put food on it for fear it will break and make a huge mess. I know it's slightly overboard to feel that way, but I really do need some time, Gray. I meant it when I said that I missed what we had, us." She shook her head. "I need a little time. Please."

Gray's face held a sad expression. "I'm not going to lose you, Sam. If it takes some time for you to think this out, that's okay. I'll wait. In the meantime, I'm hoping you'll give me a chance to see you. If you're uncomfortable about us being a couple, I do have a proposition for you."

Samantha smiled. "I can't wait to hear this," she said.

Gray looked at her with no sign of a smile. "I need help with a couple of things and since you're not needed at the museum just now, I was wondering how you'd feel about working for me and with me."

"Doing what?"

"Two different things. One, the client who has me designing the little group of shops, he wants to create a beautiful combination toy store/children's boutique. I need your input and there's a good deal of room for your creative process. He's open for suggestions and very interested in the fact that you design for a museum. Two, I'm looking for help with my house. I love the red walls you suggested, they breathe life into that room. I need your advice and even your physical abilities. Are these possibilities? Are you willing to work with me?"

Samantha thought about it for a moment then looked into Gray's eyes. "Where would I be working?"

"By my side," he said. "Sometimes at the construction site, other times in the office. Although, if you wanted to work at your grandparents' sometimes, that would be fine. As for my house, I'd like you to go through each room with your artistic eyes. Since I'm doing most of the work myself, it would be nice to have you there to do whatever you feel able to tackle. This is a paying job, Sam. I'm not looking for favors." He smiled and added, "Not yet."

Samantha took a last sip from her coffee cup. "It sounds okay, but I'd like to sleep on it overnight if you don't mind."

"I don't mind," he said.

Samantha stood and pulled her scarf closer to her neck. "I'll walk from here," she said. "It's not so cold today. How about if I give you a call tomorrow sometime with my decision?"

Gray stood and left cash on the table for the bill and the tip. "I'll be waiting to hear from you," he said. "I'm glad we bumped into each other today, Sam. Seeing you makes it all seem better somehow."

"I'll talk to you tomorrow," she said and was gone.

Chapter Eleven

Samantha said little about Gray when she returned to the home of her grandparents. She explained running into him and having a coffee with him but offered no other information. Her appetite was noticeably low at dinner and she excused herself to work upstairs in her bedroom early in the evening.

When she opened her eyes the next morning, she reached out to pat Lucy and then she began to think about Gray's proposal. She liked being busy, and she liked being around Gray. She decided quickly to work with him.

After feeding Lucy, taking a shower and getting dressed, Samantha went downstairs and walked into her grandparents' kitchen to the aroma of freshly brewed coffee and corn muffin scones.

Molly turned to look at her beautiful granddaughter. "I have your favorites," she said. "I know you love these scones and I haven't made them in a dog's age. It was time."

Samantha smiled as she poured herself a coffee and sat down at the table. "They look wonderful," she said. "I always think of Mom when I see these scones; they're her favorites too."

"You know," Molly said, "we could make a nice batch of them and send them to the vessel they're on. They get mail a couple of times a week. What do you think?"

Samantha took a bite from one of the scones and nodded. "I think they'd love them. They're so solid and good."

"Okay, then. We'll do it. Now, what are you up to today, Sweetie?"

Samantha took a swallow of coffee. "I'm actually going to be doing some work for Gray."

Molly looked surprised. "Really?"

"Yes. Well, he asked me to help him with the design for a

children's shop he's working on for a client, and he also wants some input on his own home. Since I'm out of work at the moment, I thought it would keep me busy. Do you think it's a bad idea?"

Molly laughed. "No. I think it's a fine idea. I like that boy; I think you two will work well together. When are you starting? Today?"

Samantha swallowed a small bite of the scone. "I need to call him. I wanted to think about it overnight, so I'm not positive about when I'll begin. Maybe today, I don't know."

"Well, after you finish with your breakfast, you can give him a call. I think this will be a nice couple of projects for you, Sweetie. You've always been the industrious type. And I know you'll do a fine job for him in both places."

"Thanks, Gram. Where's Gramps? He's usually planted right here in the kitchen."

"He decided to take the walk down to McHenry's for the paper. Every now and then he decides that he needs the exercise." Molly smiled and offered Samantha more coffee.

"No, thank you. I'm all set. I think I'll give Gray a call and see when and where he wants me to begin."

Sitting on the stairway out in the front hall, Samantha punched in his number and after two rings he picked up.

"Hi," she said.

"Hi," he returned. "How are you this morning?"

"Fine. I was thinking about your suggestion that I work for and with you. I've decided that would be worth giving a try."

"Good," he said. "Are you available today? I'd love to take you down to Wareham for a look. I can show you the unit they want for the children's shop; maybe you could be thinking about colors and all that. And then tonight, maybe you could join me at my house where we could have a little dinner and then appraise what should be done there. I'm anxious to get it done and move in."

Samantha took a deep breath. "Yes, I could go with you to the work site. I might as well get the feel of the place."

"And my house later?" he asked.

"May I give you the answer to that after Wareham? It will most likely work out okay, but it really depends on how long we are in Wareham."

"I have to be back for an appointment at three," he said, "so we won't be that long down there. But I'll leave it up to you. I could start a nice fire and maybe after dinner we could take a walk through each room to see what you think. It doesn't have to be a late night."

"Okay," Samantha said. "When do we leave for Wareham?"

"Okay if I pick you up in about an hour?"

Samantha shivered. "Yes. That sounds fine."

When she closed her cell phone, she sat on the steps and held it in her hand, wondering if she'd made the right decision. Everything told her that this was going to be fun and interesting, but those old feelings, the ones where she imagined everything going wrong, still surfaced. She stood and walked back into the kitchen.

"I'll be off in about an hour, Gram. Is there anything you'd like me to do before I go?"

"Not a thing, Sweetie. I'm sure Lucy is all set."

"Yes, she has fresh food and water, and before I came down this morning she was already finding birds to watch in the maple tree by my window. She loves it here."

"So," Molly began, "where are you off to?"

"Wareham. That's where Gray's client is building the fancy little shopping center, just five stores, but from Gray's description, unique. I'll take a look at the children's shop area and maybe I'll make some sketches to bring back with me. After that we're supposed to have dinner at his house and take a look at each room. He wants to move in soon."

"I'm sure he'd enjoy that. Is the place in good form? The electric and plumbing? Is it all sound?"

"He's had the necessary work done and the final piece to the puzzle is the furnace. The old one works, but not well. That's all being replaced very soon. Other than that, he's ready for the cosmetic work, which is where he'd like my input. It's such a pretty old place. I don't think there are too many homes being built with these kinds of moldings and wide board floors. Even the kitchen, Gram, you'd love it. I don't think I'd touch anything in there; it has kind of an old world charm just the way it is."

Molly smiled. "Sounds like your kind of place."

Samantha nodded. "It is. I'll enjoy adding my two cents worth."

"So, no dinner here for you tonight then?"

"No. I'll grab something with Gray. But I'll be home briefly to feed Lucy and maybe change my clothes. Gray has an appointment around three, so we won't be staying in Wareham too long."

Molly nodded and then turned away as she smiled. "Okay, Sweetie. We'll see you when you get back."

In Gray's car on the way to Wareham, about a twenty minute drive from Plymouth, he asked if she'd like to stop for a coffee or something else to drink.

"Not me," she said, "but feel free to stop if you'd like."

"I'm all set. I have you," he said and then he took his eyes from the road for just a moment to smile at his passenger.

Samantha squirmed just a bit then turned to look out at the scenery. In Wareham, Gray introduced Samantha to his clients who were there checking on the progress, and then she took her sketch book and began to wander around in the area where the children's shop would be, right in the center, with two other shops on each side. She sat down on a pile of two-by-fours and began to sketch. She worked at a corner where she imagined bookshelves and three small tables and chairs where little hands could look at books or color pictures. In the opposite corner, she made drawings of a large bed, where children could sit or lay down on their tummies to read or play with some specific soft toys. On a shelf just over the bed's headboard, she pictured stuffed animals peering down at the children. She thought about plush rugs in bright colors to lighten the fall to boney knees and tiny hands. She drew in lights that would be good to read by and others that would be good to dream by. Gray walked to her and looked over her shoulder.

"These ideas are fantastic. I think your plans will be a big hit. What child wouldn't love to spend time in a room such as this?"

Samantha looked up at him briefly then went back to her sketching. "I also envision making this room about the area. I'd love to decorate with sea shells and cranberries, maybe suspended sea gulls and Canada Geese flying overhead. There are so many options here. The space is great, and those windows to the front are going to bring in some wonderful light. I'm glad you talked me into this; it's fun."

"Where are the clothes going? I heard there's a nice line of kids' duds coming into this space."

"Over there, by the windows," Samantha said. "That would

be my choice. Of course, the owners might prefer something else, but it would really afford them the best light on the clothing while the children have their contrived world here at the back of the shop. I'll work up a few ideas for them to choose from."

"Sounds great," Gray said as he wandered around, stepping over lumber and rolls of pink insulation. "Do you have enough to work with for now? We can come back anytime we need to. I thought we might have a bite of lunch then get back to Plymouth."

Samantha stood and closed her sketchbook. "I'm ready. I have all sorts of plans swirling around in my head; I'll play with it some more at home."

Gray took her hand as she stepped over wood and tools left by the construction crew. They said goodbye to the workmen left there and headed for Gray's car.

"Anything in particular you're hoping to have for lunch? There's a little diner up ahead that has pretty good food. Their chowder is nice."

"The diner sounds good," she said.

When they arrived back in Plymouth, Gray left Samantha at her grandparents' home and went on to his office. At a little before six, he called her to ask if she was up for dinner and a stroll through his "mansion."

"Yes," she said. "Are you longing for a big meal? If sandwiches would do, Gram made meatloaf and we could have sandwiches by the fire. I also have some of Gram's chocolate chip cookies."

"Sold," he said. "I'll make some coffee and come to pick you up."

"I'll drive over," she said. "It'll just take me a few minutes to put the sandwiches together. Ketchup?"

"Absolutely. Okay then, I'll make the coffee and get the fire roaring. Thanks, Sam. I appreciate this."

Samantha closed her phone and, as always, held it in her hand as if she were holding on to Gray's hand. She smiled, ran upstairs to see Lucy and to give her some bits of meatloaf with her kibble, then made sandwiches and packed cookies into a plastic bag before saying goodbye to her grandparents and leaving for Gray's house.

Approaching the front door, she could smell the musky

sweet odor of the wood from his fireplace and she could see into the front room on the left, painted a beautiful deep cherry red. She stopped on the front path and smiled. This was going to be a very beautiful home.

With a few more steps she was at the door and touched its handle, thinking she might just walk in. Samantha hesitated and then knocked. When Gray saw her standing there, he smiled and then said, "I left it open for you. In fact, I had a key made for you so that you can come here anytime you want."

Samantha stepped inside to the warmth and slipped her coat off and into his arms. He placed it gently over a chair, then ushered her into the front room still wearing its cabbage roses. "This room needs to be next," he said. "Cabbage roses can grow in one of the other rooms, but this one, I think it needs something more simple and solid. What do you think?"

Gray had set the table in front of the fire and Samantha placed the bag containing the sandwiches and cookies down there.

"I see this room in a kind of Wedgewood blue. The moldings are already white; they could use a touch of paint, but with sheer white curtains and maybe some luscious gold drapes, this room would be so appealing and warm looking. And I can just see the Christmas tree in that front corner."

Gray laughed. "Good grief, we just got over Christmas and we're planning where to put the tree. Come on, let's eat. Ever since you mentioned Molly's meatloaf, my mouth has been watering for it. Sit down; I'll grab the coffee and a couple of mugs."

Samantha sat there looking around, thinking how wonderful it was being in this house, and with Gray. When he reentered the room with the coffee, Samantha asked, "So, this room I picture in blue, what will you use it for? The red room on the other side and this one are similar in size and shape. Either could be a parlor or a dining room. Have you figured that out yet?"

Gray poured coffee into two large mugs then set the pot down on a hot pad in the center of the table. "Well, since this room is nearer to the kitchen, I was thinking that this was probably the dining room. But, I'm not sure I want a dining room at all. I've been thinking about this room as the living room, or parlor, and the red room as a combination study and family room. The kitchen is one of my favorite places, and it's huge, so I'm thinking about a nice old country table in there and maybe some renovations to the windows. Any ideas?"

Samantha swallowed a sip of coffee and looked around as she picked up half of a meatloaf sandwich. "I like your idea of making the kitchen into the dining area. The two windows to the side could be replaced with a wonderful bay, or a square-ish box window, something that sticks out and gives you a deep window sill. Then you could put a comfy window seat there and maybe even a pair of nice rocking chairs." She smiled. "I always thought I'd have rocking chairs in my kitchen, but the kitchen I have in Boston is barely large enough to walk around in."

"So, you don't think it would be weird to do without a formal dining room?"

"Not at all. Most people use their dining rooms at holidays and as rooms to walk through to someplace else. Your kitchen could be magnificent. It's already a near perfect space."

"Okay," he said. "After we eat, we'll assess the rooms and what they need. I'll let the kitchen go for now, but I like the idea of a large window as you suggested, maybe the bay would be appropriate. That would best accommodate that window seat you mentioned."

"And the rockers."

"And the rockers," he said as he munched on his sandwich.

When their meal had been consumed except for the cookies, they walked to the rear of the house to a room opposite the large, square kitchen.

"I have no idea what they used this room for," Gray said. "When I bought the place, the realtor said she thought it had been a convenient bedroom for the woman who lived here. I guess that makes sense, and the bathroom right next door is newly done, so a bedroom is probably a good guess. I'm not so sure what I'd want to use it for though. Possibly an office."

"I think that makes good sense," Samantha said. "This is a perfect size for a computer and other office equipment. If you had clients coming here, there's even the possibility of cutting in a French door so that the entrance would be more clearly defined."

"Oh, good idea," he said. "I could just replace that one window with a door. It's a little dark back here being the northwest side of the house. What color would you suggest for in here?"

Samantha turned in a circle looking at the space. "It's darker than the front of the house, but I'd do it in green, a very soft green. Artificial lighting would take care of the room being denied sunshine except for late in the day. Green is masculine and since the lawn and gardens are out this way, I just think that the green would lend that natural feeling to the room."

Gray stood with his hands on his hips. "Yeah, I could see this room green and I like the idea of the largest part of my yard and the gardens making their way inside the house. I could get some nice houseplants for that corner over there next to where I'd probably put the door." He looked at her. "Sam, you're amazing. I see structure, but you see color and design. You're giving me some great ideas."

"Do you intend to do most of the painting yourself? I mean, if you are, I could certainly help with that. I do everything when we redecorate the museum, even pound a few nails here and there."

Gray looked at her and smiled. "You're a handy little devil."

Samantha laughed. "I like that sort of thing. It's fun."

Gray walked toward the kitchen area and she followed. "I think it's fun too. A house like this one, so filled with history, and each new owner coming along to add their personal touches, it's great. I always thought I'd build a house of my own design, but when I saw this one go up for sale, it was too much of a temptation. I'll add on to the side and the back one of these days. The screened porch off the back of the kitchen is okay for now, but it will need a complete re-haul in the near future. I see endless possibilities."

"We should have brought supplies with us," she said. "We could have painted or something."

Gray smiled. "There's lots of time for that. The new furnace is going in this week; after that, we'll paint. I suggest we have our cookies and more hot coffee, then maybe we could take a look at the four bedrooms and bathroom upstairs. I feel pretty certain it's all cosmetic stuff, but I haven't a clue as to what rooms should wear what color."

"Cookies and coffee sound good," she said. "And I already have an idea for the front bedroom, I guess that would be the master suite."

"Really? What color would you suggest for that room?"

"Aqua, very pale, just the hint of a sea sky."

Gray smiled as he poured more coffee into their mugs. "Check it out," he said. "I might need to warm it in the microwave."

Samantha took a sip. "I think so, it's barely warm."

"I'll be right back," he said as he collected the two mugs of coffee and headed to the kitchen.

When he returned and sat down, Samantha took a bite from one of the cookies and looked around the room again. "This house will be so beautiful. It already is – it's just that you'll have more of you in it when it's completed. That's what makes a house a home, personality living in every corner."

"I love the idea of the pale aqua in that upstairs bedroom. That's a favorite color of mine. Any thoughts to the other three rooms? The bathroom up there is mostly beige and white; I thought I'd leave that alone for now."

"The room in back, the one overlooking the garden area, I'll take another look, but I have the feeling that would be nice dressed in a soft gold. It's harder at night determining the colors, you almost need the natural light to lead your plans."

"That's why I'm giving you a key. I want you to be able to come here whenever you need to or want to." He stood for a moment, reached into his trouser pocket and pulled out a silver key which he handed to Samantha. "There you go. Feel free to use it whenever you wish."

"You could be sorry," she teased. "I might decide to use it when you're entertaining some sweet young thing."

Gray smiled. "What the heck, I could invite you in to join us."

"You might find yourself drenched with a garden hose," she said. "You'd better be careful."

He nodded. "I'll keep that in mind. How about if we take a quick look upstairs. And will you either go with me to the paint store or pick up some of that pale aqua for the front room? My bedroom is going to be next, I think. I can work on the rest of the house while living here."

"I'll check out the paint store tomorrow. I may need to mix the paint to get the right shade, a little white makes all the difference. Do you want to be there? I could wait to choose the color when you're available."

"I'll leave it in your capable hands. I have a busy schedule for the next few days and I'd love to get that room underway. If you could grab the paint, we could have a painting party here some night, after dinner, of course."

Samantha looked at his handsome face. "We don't need to do dinner every time we work here. I'd be fine with coming over after dinner, and even in the daytime if you're sure that's okay with you."

"I'm sure," he said.

"Okay, well how about if we take a look upstairs before we call it a night?"

"Sounds good," he said as he pushed his chair back and placed his coffee mug down on the table.

Upstairs they walked into the master bedroom and confirmed, pale aqua was the appropriate color for that space. The room at the rear of the house was determined to be best suited to gold, while the other back bedroom was allocated to being painted a warm shade of tan. Back in the other front bedroom, Samantha hesitated thinking about the right color. She thought of it in a dusty rose, but wondered if Gray would go for that.

"And this room?" he asked.

"I'm thinking," she said.

Gray walked around in the room looking at the soundness of the ceiling and touching the walls. "This would make a great nursery," he said.

Samantha looked at him and smiled. "Is there something you neglected to tell me?"

"Just that I expect to fill a nursery over and over."

Samantha found her face feeling flushed and she turned away. "Well, for now, until it's a nursery, I have a color in mind, but it may be over the top for you."

"Tell me," he said. "I'm a big strong guy; I can take it."

"Pink," she half whispered.

"Pink?"

"Kind of a dusty rose. It would be so soft in here."

Gray walked around in the room again with only the overhead light illuminating the room. "I don't know. What if we had a boy?"

Samantha looked surprised and gulped.

"Oops. I said we, didn't I? Sorry about that."

Samantha began to breathe again and then said, "If this ends up being a nursery, even the dusty rose would be okay for a boy.

Accent colors could be blue or green, and when he was older he could move into one of the other bedrooms."

Gray nodded. "Okay, I can work with that."

Samantha smiled and walked toward the bedroom door and then the staircase. "I'll finish my coffee and go along then. Tomorrow I'll check out paint colors. I won't buy anything except the aqua; I'll bring you paint chips to look at. I'm ready to get started if that's okay."

He nodded. "It's more than okay, it's great. Come on, let's have the rest of those cookies with our coffee before you go."

Samantha sat down at the small table before the hearth where embers barely seemed alive with a tiny stream of smoke.

Companionable, they both nibbled on cookies, swallowed some tepid coffee, and then Samantha stood and walked to the chair where Gray had left her coat.

"This has been fun. I'll enjoy working on your house, but right now, I'm ready for my bed."

Gray stood and smiled as he helped Samantha into her coat. "But not my bed, huh?"

Samantha stood face to face with him. "Gray," she began before he interrupted her words.

"I know," he said, "I'm on trial here. It's okay. I'll behave. I'm very grateful to have you in my life, no matter what. I was teasing about my bed, honest."

"I guess I knew that. It's just that I want to keep our work relationship on an even keel. I think we can do some wonderful things here."

"I agree completely," he said.

Outside in her car, Samantha shivered with the cold and her thoughts. Gray was unforgettable, but she still felt concerned about his emotional availability.

Chapter Twelve

The next day Samantha rolled over in her bed and saw that Lucy had helped herself to kibble. Happily watching birds in the maple tree just outside the window, the cat haphazardly cleaned her whiskers. Samantha smiled and said good morning to her. Although the greeting seemed to be more of a distraction than a courtesy to the tail-flicking feline, Samantha was used to taking a back seat to bird watching. She moved her legs from under the warm blankets and slid her feet into slippers and her arms into a robe. She made her way into the bathroom then back into the bedroom where she made her bed, gave Lucy a can of moist food and some fresh water, then went downstairs to the kitchen.

"Look who's up," Dan Elwyn said to his wife as Samantha entered the kitchen. "How are you this morning, Dear One?" he asked.

Samantha sat down as her grandmother smiled at her pretty and tousled-haired granddaughter. "Hi, Sweetie. Tea or coffee to start?"

"Oh, tea, I think. I'll get it, Gram."

"No need, it's all ready. I made a pot of tea and a pot of coffee: I was in that mood. So," she said as she placed a cup and saucer before Samantha, "here you are."

"I'm getting spoiled," Samantha said. "It's going to feel so empty when I go back to my place in Boston. I'm lucky to have a cup of anything before I go to work, and certainly not homemade cinnamon buns and corn muffin scones."

"It's good to get spoiled sometimes," her grandfather said.

"And you know that firsthand," Molly said with a smile.

Dan Elwyn winked at his wife then asked Samantha what her plans were for the day.

"One of my goals today is to pick up some aqua paint for one of the rooms in Gray's house. I'm helping him to get the place in shape; I'll do some painting there while he's at work. Is there something I could do for either one of you? I'd be more than happy to do whatever I can to help." Samantha smiled at her grandparents and continued, "I can't allow myself to be a freeloader, you know."

"There's no way in the world we'd ever consider you that," Molly said. "It's wonderful having you around. I'm going to dread having you return to Boston."

"Now you said aqua paint. Where's this going? Which room?" Dan Elwyn asked.

"His bedroom," Samantha said. "We did a walkthrough the house last night and made decisions on the colors. It's going to be beautiful."

"With you providing the decorating, I have no doubt," Molly said.

Samantha took a sip of her tea then asked, "So, is there something I can do to help out here?"

"Not a thing," Molly said.

After giving her bedroom a quick vacuuming, Samantha dressed in jeans and a brown jersey, brushed her hair, then headed downstairs to retrieve her coat, keys and purse. She said goodbye to her grandparents then went off to the paint store. She found a soft aqua color, bought white to mix with it if needed, then drove to Gray's house. It felt strange to slip the key in the lock, a little invasive, but once inside she felt perfectly at home.

Samantha smiled at the thought of making herself a cup of hot tea to drink as she worked. She slipped out of her coat and gloves and left them on a chair Gray often used in place of a front hall closet.

In the kitchen, she ran water from the faucet into a mug with a tea bag then set it in the microwave for two minutes. She looked around at the white walls, the copper pots hanging over a center island. It was perfect. A good scrubbing might be in order but, other than that, it had the old world look that Gray and she loved.

As the microwave beeped, finished with making tea, Samantha felt a little pang of regret that this wonderful old house wasn't hers. She blew gently at the hot tea then felt her lips form a smile as she walked toward the front room where she'd left the paint supplies. The future was definitely an unknown, and she wasn't planning on anything, but the possibilities were there. Maybe this wonderful old place could one day be her home as well as Gray's; a pleasant dream if nothing else.

She took the two cans of paint upstairs along with brushes, a roller, a paint pan, a large drop cloth to protect the wide pine floors, and a variety of little helper tools. She pried open the top of the aqua and dabbed a foot long streak on the wall toward the sea. Too vivid, she decided. With a paint stick, she measured into the pan about two thirds aqua to one third white, mixing it with a back and forth swirling until the color was muted and soft. Another foot long streak on the walls proved to be exactly what she'd hoped for and she began to paint.

By the time she sipped at her tea, it was cold and she looked at her watch to see that after painting two walls, three hours had passed. Being just after two in the afternoon, she was thinking she'd enjoy a nice sandwich or a bowl of soup as her cell phone rang.

Samantha looked at the phone and saw that the caller was Gray. "Hi," she said.

"Hey, are you at the house?"

Samantha smiled. "I told you I would be. You should see the paint, the pale aqua. It's positively dreamy. I think you're going to like waking up in this room."

"Oh really? Maybe I should pop over there and take a look."

"Now?"

"That's what I'm thinking. Any reason I shouldn't?" he asked.

"No, of course not. But if you're coming, will you bring me something to eat? I'm starved."

"No problem. What would you like? Thai, Mexican? And do you need a drink?"

"No drink, I have tea I can reheat. And just a sandwich of some sort would be great."

"Okay. I'll hit the deli and I'll be over. Make me a cup of tea too?"

Samantha smiled. "I'll do that."

When the call ended, she found herself holding the phone again, keeping him close. She hadn't exhibited this strange behavior with anyone else, not ever. Gray was having a powerful effect on her, which she felt was both wonderful and frightening.

When he walked into the house, Samantha was sitting in the

kitchen, enjoying warm tea and the view of the back gardens.

"Dinner is served," he said with a smile as he handed her a brown deli bag.

Samantha opened it and found a turkey and lettuce sandwich on dark bread; two chocolate cupcakes were in a clear box below.

She smiled as she unwrapped the sandwich. "Want half?"

"No thanks, but one of those cupcakes has my name on it."

Samantha stood as she munched on her sandwich. "Come on," she said as she moved toward the stairway. "I want you to see your bedroom."

They climbed the stairs and entered the first room on the left, the largest of the four rooms on that level.

"Wow," he said with his hands on his hips. "This is magnificent. You sure know your colors, Sam. Nothing else would ever have measured up to this."

"I'm glad you like it. I think it will be pretty at night too, with soft lighting."

"Amazing," he said as he looked at her bright eyes. "Come on, let's get back downstairs to your sandwich and those cupcakes."

In the kitchen, Samantha stood and reached for the second half of her sandwich. "Are you sure you wouldn't like some of this?"

"I'm sure," he said. "I had a meal with the folks from Wareham; they're very excited about this building project. I told them about some of your ideas for the children's shop and they'd definitely like you involved with the plans."

Samantha took a few sips of her tea to wash down a bite of her sandwich. "That sounds like fun. Did you tell them I'm slightly preoccupied with working for a gentleman in Plymouth just now?"

Gray smiled. "No, but they're not ready for you yet anyway. By the way, what are we doing about compensating you for the work you're doing here? You wanted to keep this as a business agreement, so let's decide on your salary. What did they pay you at the museum?"

Samantha looked almost injured. "Gray, I have no intention of taking a salary of any kind from you. I offered to do the painting; I like it, and I feel privileged that you're willing to share the restoration of this wonderful place with me."

"Sam, you've got to be kidding. I can't have you working here for nothing."

"It's not for nothing. You brought me lunch."

He looked at her and shook his head from side to side. "I'm not winning this debate, am I?"

"No, afraid not."

"Okay. So does the cat like caviar?"

Samantha laughed. "I have no idea and I never will. That's all I need is a snooty cat. No caviar."

"All right. What are you doing this weekend?"

"I don't know. Why?"

"Remember the friend I told you about, the attorney who lives with his wife in Providence?"

"Yes, Paul, wasn't it?"

"Paul and Kate. They called yesterday and asked when I was coming down. I told them about you and they'd love to meet you. Are you available on Saturday or Sunday?"

"If I'm not working here, sure."

"Hey, I'm no slave driver. You can take the weekends off. First thing Monday though, I'll expect you back on the site."

"Yes, sir," she said.

"So, which day would you like to go?"

"I'm flexible," she said.

"Okay. Then how about if we take in a movie or something Saturday night and go off to Providence on Sunday? They've invited us to dinner whenever we visit."

"Aren't you monopolizing my entire weekend?"

"That would be correct," he said.

Samantha thought about it for a moment then smiled. "Okay."

When the weekend came, Samantha had finished painting the pale aqua in the front room and had painted one of the back bedrooms a mellow gold. Their Saturday evening consisted of dinner, a movie, a stroll along the harbor, then delivering Samantha back at her grandparents' just after midnight.

At the door, Gray pulled Samantha close to him and bent down enough to kiss the soft tissue at the side of her neck. She shivered and, as she did so, his lips pressed firmly against her own and they stood locked in that embrace for several minutes, neither of them wanting to pull away.

"Tomorrow," he said as he finally managed to put an inch of space between Samantha and himself.

"Tomorrow," she said.

Sunday morning brought sunshine to Samantha's room as she opened her eyes. Lucy was stretched out next to her and, as always, Samantha reached out to give the cat a gentle pat. She swung her legs from the covers of the bed, moved her feet into slippers and her arms into a soft robe. Downstairs she found her grandparents in the kitchen, her grandfather reading *The Boston Sunday Globe* and her grandmother sipping coffee as she made a grocery list.

"Good morning," she greeted them happily.

They both returned the greeting to her and then Molly asked what Samantha would enjoy for breakfast. There were scrambled eggs all ready to be warmed and toast easily made in a moment.

"I think I'll have those eggs, Gram. That sounds good, but stay where you are; I'm perfectly capable of warming them in the microwave."

"You sound very chipper this morning," Dan Elwyn said.

Samantha smiled at them both. "I'm off on a bit of an adventure today. Gray invited me to Providence to meet an old college friend and his wife. And look at the sunshine out there: it's a crisp, beautiful day."

Molly smiled at Dan before giving her attention to Samantha. "That sounds wonderful, Sweetie. How nice to be meeting Gray's friend."

"Yes," Dan Elwyn agreed. "A man doesn't take a woman to meet friends unless he's getting mighty serious."

Samantha took a bite of her eggs and looked hesitant to reply. Molly spoke to ease the tension. "No jumping to conclusions now, Daniel. Gray is rightly proud of Samantha, that's all. Leave the poor girl alone."

When Samantha felt that she could safely speak, she placed her fork down on the plate and said, "I hope you don't mind that I won't be here for Sunday dinner. We're leaving around noon and I doubt we'll be back before six or seven this evening."

"That's perfectly fine, Sweetie. Go and have a good time," Molly said.

Shortly after eleven, Samantha chose a pair of charcoal gray slacks and a soft black tunic style shirt to wear. With her hair brushed and shining, and Gray's shell necklace in place, she slipped her feet into black flat-heeled shoes. She said goodbye to Lucy and, back downstairs, she chatted with her grandparents until she heard the knock at the door.

"Hi," he said as his eyes appraised her from head to toe.

"Hi," she said, her eyes taking in his jeans, pale blue shirt and bomber jacket. He looked incredibly handsome. "Come on in," she invited. "I'll grab my coat if you'd like to say hello to Gram and Gramps; they're in the parlor."

After a few minutes of pleasant exchanges between Gray, Molly and Dan, Samantha appeared in the parlor doorway, her long coat and shoulder purse on and ready to go.

"I'll take good care of her," Gray said to the two older people.

"I'm sure you will," Dan Elwyn said with a wink to Samantha, and with a quick kiss to each of her grandparents, Samantha and Gray were on their way.

In the car and about to turn onto the highway, Gray looked at Samantha and asked, "So, are you ready?"

She smiled and said that she was.

"Ah," he said, "but are you prepared for me to take full possession of you? Are you game for being kidnapped and contained?"

Samantha gave him a raised eyebrow and kept silent.

He laughed. "Don't look so worried. We're just going to Paul and Kate's. Not that it wouldn't be pleasant to steal you away. Would you like to grab a coffee or tea for the trip? There's a coffee shop at the next exit."

"That sounds good," she said and, within minutes, they stopped at a drive-thru for two coffees. Back on the road, they enjoyed a light as well as interesting conversation and forty-five minutes later, they arrived in Providence. They pulled into the driveway of a large Victorian home, painted sage green with salmon trim.

"This is so pretty," Samantha said as the car came to a halt and Gray turned off the engine.

After introductions and being invited to sit by a marble fireplace aglow with a warm blaze, Paul presented a bottle of wine brought by Gray and four glasses.

"Three wines, one apple juice, coming up," he said cheerfully as he gently patted his wife's protruding abdomen.

Samantha smiled at them both. Kate's hair was almost black

and back in a long ponytail, while Paul's hair was pale blonde. It would be interesting to see the hair color of their soon expected baby.

"After we have our drinks," Kate said to Samantha, "I'll show you the house and then we can let the guys have a few minutes while I put an appetizer together in the kitchen."

"I'd love to see the house," Samantha said, "and if there's anything I can do in the kitchen, I'd be happy to help."

With drinks enjoyed, Kate offered Samantha the promised tour. They explored the first floor and then the second before climbing the stairway to the attic: a large, open space, bright and inviting.

"This is a fabulous room, Kate. I'd be up here all the time."

"We love it. It's a great family room set up. I have to admit, I favor the rooms downstairs because I love the hearths, but for a child to muck about with his or her toys, this is a great space in which to play. Gray told us that you design rooms for children in a Boston museum. That sounds very playful."

Samantha smiled as they made their way back down two flights of stairs to the kitchen. "It is playful, I love it. My only issue is that I really dread going back to my place in Boston. I'm very attached to Plymouth, and living at my grandparents' home is wonderful."

"Gray told us the museum is under some renovations," Kate said as she reached for a tray on which to place a variety of vegetables and a dip.

"That's right," Samantha said. "It could be a few weeks before they open again. Can I help in any way, Kate?"

"Sure, how about if you mix the dip. Here's the sour cream and the herbs to go in it, and then there are some crackers over in that cupboard over there. We can add a few of them to the vegetable tray."

Samantha went to the cupboard and found a box of crackers which she brought back to the center island.

"So," Kate began, "you and Gray are a good fit it seems."

Samantha smiled as she mixed the dip. "He's an interesting man," she said.

"And that's an important feature," Kate said. "I've known so many people who get hooked on a person's looks, or their career, or some crazy attraction, but in the long-run, having someone interesting to talk with is pretty important. I swear Paul and I are like twins. Of course, I went with a few weird ones, but once I met Paul, I knew I was home."

Samantha looked at Kate and smiled. "That's a nice way to put it, *home*."

"So," Kate asked with a little grin on her cute face, "are you home?"

Samantha could feel the blush arriving in her cheeks. "We're pretty new," she said.

"Uh-huh, but sometimes home is felt pretty quickly."

"He's special," Samantha finally said, not sure how much she wanted to reveal of her feelings.

"Well," Kate began, "Gray's never brought anyone here before. And I can tell you that even when the excitement and rush of having that new person in your life is settling down, it's the person's demeanor, their thought for the relationship, that gets us through. Paul is my man, plain and simple."

Samantha enjoyed the easy conversation in the kitchen with Kate, and then the laughter and old college stories around the dining room table with Paul and Gray telling the tales.

On their way back to Plymouth that evening, Gray asked, "Did you like Kate and Paul? I think they liked you a lot."

"They're great. Kate is my type of person, very down to earth and bright. I like Paul too; he has a good sense of humor, and I love the way he pampers Kate."

"He's crazy about her. He went with a girl our freshman year in college and she was a heartbreaker. She cheated on him and it took a while for him to gain trust again, even though he wouldn't admit it. Kate was exactly what he needed."

Samantha nodded. "I can see that they're an exemplary couple, and they're both so excited about the baby."

"That's going to be one very happy baby. Paul is already planning what college he thinks this child should attend."

Samantha laughed. "He's nice. Thank you for taking me to meet them; I had a good time."

Gray looked at her and smiled. "They thanked me for bringing you along. I can see a long-term bond forming from this day."

Samantha made no comment, but it sounded very much like Gray was suggesting a future with not only Paul and Kate, but with them. Could that happen? She wanted to think so, but she was still wary of letting down her guard. The Karrys of the world were out there, and she still could envision Gray dancing with that girl on his birthday.

"Penny for your thoughts," he said, noting her quietness.

When she still said nothing, he asked, "Are you still thinking about Karry? Because if you are, Sam, there's nothing to think about. In fact, I was ecstatic to see you wearing your shell today. I was worried when I saw that you didn't other times."

"She's fading," Samantha said.

"Good, because even if there was no Samantha Elwyn in my world, there would absolutely be no Karry."

"Who have you been drawn to over the years? I can't imagine that there wasn't someone."

Gray's facial muscles moved just a bit as she glanced at his handsome profile. "I dated a few. One in particular was interesting. She was a med student, very into that portion of her life. I liked her, she liked me, but medicine was her greatest love. I admired her for that, but it wasn't where I was going. It ended and for the best."

"How long ago was that?" Samantha asked, worried that he might still be carrying the torch.

"Oh, five, maybe six years ago. What about you? Who shook the peaches from your tree?"

Samantha laughed. "One or two. I was always a little leery of boys' attentions. A friend of mine started warning me when I was about thirteen that all the boys wanted was a physical connection. That troubled me. I had the occasional boyfriend, but until I began to date one in particular, I didn't allow myself to get too involved."

"What happened with him?"

Samantha shifted a bit in her seat watching the scenery go by. "I came to the conclusion that we were treading water. There was no chemistry. He was a very nice, intelligent person, but other than going to the Pops or to see some play at the Wang Center, we really had no catch, no electricity."

Gray was the quiet one this time, but Samantha took note of the look on his face, one of relief.

When they neared Plymouth, Gray asked if she'd like to have a nightcap someplace before going home.

"I'd love to," she said, "as long as that's agreeable to you."

"Absolutely. Where would you like to go? The town is at

our beck and call."

"Do you have anything at your house?" she asked.

Gray glanced at her and smiled. "I have a couple of bottles of wine, some brandy, soda, coffee and tea. Any of that interest you?"

"Yes. A cup of coffee would be great. I plan to work at the house tomorrow, and I want to check to make sure that I have enough painter's tape. I've been very careful not to get paint on the moldings."

"I noticed," he said. "You're meticulous when it comes to painting. I'm sure I would have made a mess of it myself."

Samantha enjoyed the drive from Providence and, more so, the drive through Plymouth Center to Gray's driveway.

"We're home," he said as he looked over at her and switched the engine off.

Chapter Thirteen

"Should I start a fire?" Gray asked as the two entered the front room.

Samantha was thinking that he'd started a fire a long time ago, in her heart.

"Probably not," she said. "It's late and since we're both working tomorrow, it might be best to pass on the crackling hearth this time. And you won't hear me say that too often; I love using the fireplace in a home. I just want to check on the tape. I'll run upstairs and make sure I'm set to come here in the morning."

Gray smiled at her enthusiasm and walked into the kitchen as she left the room and approached the stairway. He looked around, loving the way a dim light cast shadows on the white walls, giving them soft streaks of pale gray. He walked back into the front room as Samantha came down the stairs.

"I have everything all ready," she said with a smile. "Guess what I intend to do before I come here though."

Gray cocked his head to one side. "By the look on your face, I'm not sure I want to know."

Samantha laughed. "Well, if you're still willing, I'm going to buy the dusty rose paint for the other front room and get started on it. I can't wait. I know it's going to be spectacular."

Gray smiled. "I'm willing and I'm sure it will be just as eye catching as you suggest. The idea is actually settling in with me very well. My mother can't wait to see it."

Samantha smiled. "She's probably a little surprised, right?"

"Yes, I'd say so. And Dad, well, he's more than surprised."

Samantha laughed. "Wait until they see it. If you don't love it when it's finished, there's this fabulous invention we can apply. It's called paint. We can always change the color."

"I trust your opinion completely. I'll be looking forward to seeing it tomorrow around noon when I bring your lunch."

Samantha laughed. "You don't really have to bring me lunch," she said. "I can bring a sandwich from Gram's kitchen."

"Oh no," he said. "I'm bringing us lunch. Do you have a preference?"

"No," she said.

"Okay then. I'll surprise you some time between noon and one. Is it okay if I call it a date since you insist on this being a business arrangement?"

"It's a date," she said with a smile. "Now, how about if you deliver me home where I can get a good night's rest and see Lucy. That poor cat, I'm sure she thinks I've abandoned her."

"Maybe you should get her a hamster to keep her company," he suggested with a twinkle in his eyes.

"Don't go there," she warned.

Together they left the house, leaving a few lights on low with the touch of a dimmer switch. Within moments they stopped before her grandparents' home and, before she could tell him there was no need to get out of the car, he was out and opening her door.

As they walked toward the entrance to the kitchen, Gray took hold of her hand and, when they stopped, he pressed her palm to his chest.

"Feel that heart in there?" he asked softly.

Samantha looked up into his handsome face and said nothing.

"Every beat of that heart, every molecule flowing through this body, has Samantha Elwyn energy to thank."

She smiled and turned her head up to lightly kiss his lips. "I'll see you tomorrow for lunch," she said.

Gray kissed her with more emphasis than she'd expected, then released her as he moved toward his car. Then he stopped, turned around and said, "Hey, what about the paint? I need to give you some cash."

"No," she said. "They've been putting the supplies on your account. Mr. Silverman said that you're in there all the time and there was no reason to pay on the spot. I hope that's okay."

Gray smiled. "It's more than okay and it's accurate. Zak Silverman must be getting a kick out of this though. He's always at me about women. Now that you're my personal decorator, I'm sure he's got the wedding planned."

Samantha felt her body tighten, but she liked the feeling. "Goodnight, Gray. See you tomorrow."

Gray smiled and turned away toward his car as Samantha opened the door to her grandmother's warm kitchen.

The next morning, after routine tasks were completed, Samantha made her way to the paint store where she purchased a gallon of paint called Winter Rose. She loved the depth and softness of the color and felt certain that if it needed to be lightened, the gallon of white she'd purchased to go with the aqua would work well. While there, she also purchased a gallon of paint for the other bedroom to the rear of the house. A muted putty color; Samantha could envision that room with amber lights and soft, afternoon sun filtering in. Armed with paint sticks for mixing and two plastic buckets, she happily left Mr. Silverman's store with him teasing her about being the prettiest painter he'd ever seen.

By ten o'clock, Samantha had begun to paint the front bedroom in its wonderful shade of rose. She stood back and looked at the four-foot area she'd completed, confident that she'd chosen the best color for that room, without having to have added any white.

At just after noon, she heard footsteps downstairs and stood, admiring the walls she had painted. She walked to the top of the staircase where she saw Gray approaching.

"Hi," he said. "I'm quivering with anticipation. May I take a look?"

Samantha smiled. "Certainly, come on up."

Gray climbed the stairs and she moved aside to let him pass into the rose painted room. She watched his expression as his eyes scanned the wall she had completed.

"This is beautiful," he said as he turned and looked at her with awe in his eyes.

"I told you," she said as she dipped her brush into a jar of water.

Gray turned and looked at the wall again, then back at Samantha. "I trusted you with this and I was right. It's so warm. Wow, I'm really blown away with this. I love it."

Samantha cleaned her hands with a rag then dropped it next to her other supplies.

"Ready for lunch?" he asked.

"I'm starved," she said. "And I desperately need a cup of tea or coffee. I don't know why, but I started in working without one and I miss my caffeine."

"Come on down," he beckoned. "I'll make us a pot of something, what do you prefer?"

"Coffee, I think," she said as they made their way down the stairway.

"Sit down," he said."I'll just get the coffee started."

Samantha looked at the little table where they always ate before the hearth. It was set with two paper plates, three containers which looked and smelled like Thai food, a fork to the left, a knife and spoon to the right, and in the center of it all, a bouquet of bright yellow daffodils. She smiled at his thoughtfulness.

"The coffee's on," he said as he walked back into the room. "Would you like some water or a soda until we have the coffee?"

"Oh," she said, "water might be good. I'll get it."

Gray put his hand up and gestured for her to stay. "I'm up, I'll get two waters and I'll be right back. Help yourself to the food; I hope I made choices you'll enjoy."

"No bad choices with Thai," she said. "It smells delicious."

When he returned with the water, Samantha thanked him and commented on the flowers. "These are wonderfully cheerful," she said.

"Good. I wanted to bring you something to match your personality."

Samantha smiled as she swallowed a sip of water and then placed her glass down on the table. "You always say exactly the right thing."

Gray looked up as he sat down across from her. "I've never tried harder."

"Why?" she asked as she scooped some rice onto her plate.

"Sam," he said with his spoon in mid-air, "isn't it even slightly obvious that I'm trying to make my very best impression here?"

Samantha helped herself to a soft roll and then some vegetables with noodles.

"Well, you're succeeding when it comes to food," she said. "This looks so good."

Gray looked at her. "I'm thinking about a lot more than the food," he said.

"Yes, but this is business, remember?" she teased and then inserted a forkful of food into her mouth.

"Okay, Lady," he said as he reached for the rice. "I'm going to let you get away with this bossy attitude for a while, but when this painting stuff is done, watch out."

"Thanks for the warning," she said.

"I'll be right back. That coffee should be ready by now."

She watched him move, his lean form attractive in navy blue trousers, a white shirt with its sleeves rolled back to the elbows and a pale blue tie covering the shirt's buttons.

When he returned with the coffee in ample mugs, Samantha reached for hers and took a sip. "Oh, this is so good. I've been wishing for a nice hot drink all morning. Thank you."

Gray sat down across from her and smiled. "My pleasure."

"By the way," she began as she placed her fork down on the plate. "I bought the paint for the other back bedroom too. It's pretty much what we discussed, a soft gray-brown color called putty. I hope that's still okay."

"I have complete trust in every move you make. I didn't have a clue as to what color any of these rooms should be. That other room downstairs in red, that was a surprise to me how wonderful that looks. Can't wait to get started with that blue you suggested in this room. What did you refer to it as?"

"Kind of a Wedgewood blue. Maybe even slightly deeper. This room gets the full morning sun, so it can definitely handle the rich blue."

"Great," he said. "Now, just to intrude ever so slightly on this business deal we have going, what's the scoop for our social lives? Are you too tired to go out at night? Could we make some tentative plans for the weekend? I was wondering if you had any interest in heading off to New Hampshire or Maine for an overnight. Spring is in the air. I think this time of year would be pretty up there. How about it?"

Samantha looked at him with a straight face as she held her coffee mug just above the table. "Over night?"

Gray looked at her. "Uh-huh. It would depend on where we went, of course, but if we head up very far, it would be nice to stay over."

Samantha took a sip of the hot coffee and said nothing.

"Cat got your tongue?" he asked and then smiled. "Sorry. No offense to Lucy, I know she wouldn't get your tongue."

Samantha placed her mug down and looked out through a window then back at Gray's face.

"I suppose it seems a little strange being in my late twenties, but I haven't ever gone overnight with anyone. Not anywhere."

Gray looked at her and sat forward, his elbows on the table.

"Sam. Most places have separate rooms available. I wasn't making an indecent proposal. I just thought the trip would be fun, and we deserve some fun, don't we?"

"I guess. I'll think about it. Okay," she said spontaneously. "Let's do it."

Gray laughed. "You decided that quick, huh? Okay, I'm holding you to it. This Saturday morning we'll head north to parts unknown. Think about where you'd like to go, the sky's the limit."

"Oh," she said, "I know where we could go. Mom and Dad took us one time to this place in Vermont. The town is called Quechee and they have this beautiful gorge there. We could hike around a little bit, and then, not far from there, there's the town of Woodstock. I love that place, it's so quaint. Could we go there?"

Gray smiled. "Of course we could. I've been through Quechee on the way to Rutland a couple of times. Never had time to enjoy the place, so this will be great. I'm glad you thought of it."

"And if we travel over on Route Four to Rutland, we can go south to Bennington and then back toward home. That would be an amazing journey, Gray. It's been years and years since I've done that."

Gray smiled at Samantha's enthusiasm. "Can't wait," he said.

When Gray left to go back to his office, Samantha continued painting the rose-colored room then heated herself another cup of coffee. It was around four in the afternoon when she decided to see how she liked the putty color on the walls of the back room. With a corner painted, displaying the near-to-sunset light on two walls, Samantha stood back a few feet and decided that it had a cozy affect, perfect for that room. She sealed the cans of paint, washed her brushes, and prepared to lock the house as she slipped her arms into her coat and her hands into gloves. She was pleased. The house was coming alive with care and thought-filled attention to the light in each room.

She rinsed her coffee mug out and set it to dry next to Gray's then, with one last look around, she switched on a light here and there, locking the door before she left.

Samantha drove to her grandparents' home, her heart light and her mind thinking about the weekend trip to Vermont. She couldn't wait to tell them.

After poking her gloves into her pockets, she hung her coat in the front hallway closet and made her way into the kitchen where her grandmother was placing a chicken pot pie into the oven.

"Hi, Sweetie," Molly said. "You had a long day over at Gray's; you must be tired out by now."

"Not really," Samantha said, "but I'm looking forward to an evening at home. I'm thinking I might bring Lucy down tonight too, if that's okay with you."

"Of course it is," Molly said. "I do have something to tell you though."

Samantha looked at her grandmother's serious expression. "Is there something wrong, Gram?"

"Well, it's not anything terribly serious, Dear, but the fact is your brother Kyle has been in an accident. Peter called about an hour ago to tell us."

"Oh no," Samantha said. "Where is he? Is he in a hospital? What are the injuries? How did it happen?"

Dan Elwyn entered the kitchen. "Bad news, eh, Sweetheart? This is the tough part about living so far apart."

"He's in the hospital," Molly said. "Peter told me that the injuries aren't severe, but he'll need to be there for a few days before they let him go home. And then what? He lives alone; I wonder how he'll manage."

Samantha sat down in a kitchen chair and felt stunned. "I should go," she said. "I'll make a reservation to leave tomorrow. With Mom and Dad out to sea, they can't get back; he should have someone with him."

"What about his girlfriend?" Dan Elwyn suggested.

"We don't know anything about her," Samantha said. "And actually, when it comes to something like this, family should step in. It might be awkward for a girlfriend to help him to the bathroom or something like that. I'll go. There's no choice."

"You don't think Peter could handle it, Sweetie?" Molly asked.

"I'll talk to Peter later," Samantha said, "but he has a job; I doubt he'd be able to take the time off."

By the end of the evening, it was all arranged. Samantha would fly to California to see her brothers. She and Peter would see to Kyle's needs once he came home, and they would determine how much care he'd require at that time.

At nine that evening, Samantha called Gray to tell him that she'd be away for a week or so. Concerned, he told her that if there was anything he could do, she should let him know. He'd be waiting to see her when she came back home.

"The idea of you being so far away is troubling," he said. "I'll miss you, Sam."

That night, Samantha left Lucy with her grandparents and drove into Boston. At her apartment, she packed one carry-on bag with clothes enough to get by for at least a week, jerseys and jeans that would easily wash and be worn again. In the morning she drove to Logan Airport and boarded a plane bound for Los Angeles. Peter met her there and drove her to the hospital where she found Kyle bruised and bandaged with his injuries.

"You are one very sorry sight," she said to her brother.

"It hurts to smile," he mumbled. "So, thanks for the compliment."

"Peter told me that you were a passenger in the car that was hit. I'm really sorry, Kyle. This is awful."

Kyle closed his eyes then opened them to look at his pretty sister. "I'll be okay," he said.

Within three days, Kyle was able to leave the hospital using crutches for a broken ankle and three other shattered bones in his left foot.

"I talked to Katie earlier," Peter said as he and Samantha drove Kyle home. "She's bringing dinner over tonight for the three of you."

"The three?" Samantha asked. Looking at Kyle she said, "No way. I'll go out for a while and give the two of you some alone time. Don't worry, Kyle. I won't be a hovering sister, I promise."

"Are you kidding?" Kyle said. "I've never been so glad to see anyone in my life. I can't even tell you how much I appreciate you coming all this way to help out, Sam. Katie and Peter have their work; they aren't available. You being here makes all the difference."

"Hey," Peter began, "how about if you and I have a pizza together tonight?" he asked Samantha. "There's also this independent film showing at the Fairway Theatre downtown. Any interest? It's supposed to be very good."

"Absolutely," Samantha said. "I'd love pizza and a film."

Between needing therapy for his left elbow and shoulder, his inabilities with his broken foot and other injuries, the days faded into one another and, before long, two weeks had passed. Samantha assured her parents who were near Bali on their ship that Kyle was mending well. She spoke daily with her grandparents and was assured that they and Lucy were doing fine.

"You wouldn't believe it," Molly said. "Gray showed up here last evening with a dish of broiled scallops and a catnip mouse for Lucy."

Samantha's eyes filled with tears. "He's pretty nice," she managed to say.

That evening she called Gray and he picked up the phone immediately.

"I never thought time would stand still," he said, "but since you left Plymouth, it has. I miss you like crazy."

Samantha could detect the sincerity in his voice. "I miss you too. Gram told me about you bringing scallops and the mouse to Lucy. Are you trying to win her over so that she cares more for you than for me?"

Gray laughed. "You figured me out."

Samantha scattered moisture from her eyes. "Thought so," she said.

"Have you figured out that I am totally saturated with feelings for you? All I've been able to think about is why I haven't pinned you to a wall and told you what you mean to me. I'm scared to death of losing you. And I can't wait to see you."

Samantha swallowed hard and looked around the living room in her brother's apartment.

"I can't wait to get back," she said.

"How's Kyle doing?" he asked.

"Better. He's getting around well with the crutches, and between Katie and Peter, I think he's going to manage okay without me in another couple of days. I'm hoping to catch a flight home next weekend. Unfortunately, I won't be able to stay in Plymouth long. I've spoken with my boss, Julie, at the museum. They're ready for me to start decorating."

"So you won't be living in Plymouth?"

"Not for a little while. I'll go back there and collect Lucy, but I need to fulfill my obligations with the museum. After this, I'm going to give my notice. I'll live with Gram and Gramps while I finish my book, then I'll see what I can find for work in the Plymouth area. This accident of Kyle's has made me realize all the more that I need to do what's best, and what's best is living where I love the people and the place."

"Hey," he said, "any chance I'd be one of those people?"

Samantha smiled and held the phone to her lips. "Maybe," she said.

The next day as Samantha prepared eggs over easy for her brother, Katie walked into the apartment with freshly baked croissants from a local bakery.

"They smell fantastic," Samantha said. "I have coffee all made and Kyle's eggs are about ready. How would you like yours?"

"Are you having some?" Katie asked.

"I was thinking of scrambled, but I could make some for you and then leave to give you and Kyle some alone time."

"No," she said, "please stay. I'll have scrambled eggs with you. I'd really like the chance to get to know you as much as I can. I plan to marry your brother, you know."

Samantha laughed. "I didn't know for sure. When did he propose?"

Katie took a bite of buttered croissant and said, "He didn't. I'm sick of waiting for him; I'm proposing to him. And he'll say yes, I know he will."

Samantha laughed again. "Katie, you're a riot. I think you're perfect for Kyle, and he'd be absolutely nuts not to accept your proposal."

Katie nodded as she chewed. "I'm an independent woman. I have a good, secure job, I have money in the bank for a down payment on something like a condo or a small house, and I adore your brother. I'm qualified."

Samantha smiled and then hugged Katie. "I couldn't be happier," she said.

"What about you?" Katie asked. "Kyle told me there's someone in your life back in Massachusetts."

"Yes," Samantha said, "there is."

"And is he wonderful?"

"Yes."

"And is he handsome and incredibly sexy?"

"Yes."

"Okay then," Katie said. "What in the world are you doing here in California? I can work with Peter to take care of Kyle. He's doing great; you know that. Go home to your life, Samantha. Honestly, I can't wait to go there myself with Kyle to meet your grandparents and see the east coast. My family is here, this is home, but it sounds so wonderful out where you live."

Samantha nodded. "It is."

Over the next several days, Samantha cleaned Kyle's apartment, did three loads of laundry, washed windows and curtains, and stocked his refrigerator with home-baked brownies, cookies, and other favorite foods. He was able to work on his computer during the day and managed the crutches well enough to allow him to live on his own. Everyone agreed it was time for Samantha to resume her life in Massachusetts.

When she arrived at Logan, she drove to her apartment where she showered and changed into fresh clothing. It was early evening when Samantha decided to drive to Plymouth, pick up Lucy and a few of her personal items, and then prepare to go into the museum the next day. She called her grandparents to tell them she was on her way, then she called Gray. He did not answer her call, but she understood that he could be out with a client; it was only about seven-thirty.

At her grandparents' home, she hugged them both a long time, told them all about Kyle and how wonderful Katie was, then she noticed that Lucy was sleeping in a padded chair by the table.

"Hey," she said to the drowsy cat. "How about a hello for me?" Samantha rubbed Lucy's ears and the cat opened her eyes lazily to look at her friend.

"I hope you don't mind, Sweetie. We thought she might be lonely upstairs by herself so much. We brought her down and she seems to like it. We've been very careful about the doors. No chance she'd get out."

"I'm glad you brought her down. Poor thing, she's going to hate going back to Boston now."

"Must she go?" Dan Elwyn asked. "If you're serious about giving up the job at the museum and your apartment in the city, wouldn't it be better to leave her here?"

"Now, Dan," Molly began, "Lucy's Samantha's cat, not yours."

Samantha smiled. "I think she's *ours*. She's so content here. What do you think, Gram? Should I let her stay with you until I find a place of my own down this way? I'd miss her, but she seems so settled, I hate to plop her in the apartment, especially since I'll be packing things up soon. Would she be an inconvenience?"

"Oh no," Molly said. "We love having Lucy around. She's no problem at all."

That settled, Samantha had a sandwich with chicken dinner leftovers and then tried calling Gray again. Still no answer. Before going back into Boston, Samantha checked her room to see if it needed tidying, packed a few clothes she would take home to wash, then returned to the kitchen where her grandparents sat with Lucy.

"Did Gray know you were coming down to Plymouth?" Dan Elwyn asked.

"No. I thought I'd surprise him, but I guess the surprise is on me. He must be with a client. I'll call him when I get back to the apartment. I'm so tired, I think I need a good night's sleep."

With a gentle patting for Lucy and hugs to her grandparents, Samantha reluctantly left Plymouth and drove back to Boston. Once there, she hung her coat in a closet, kicked off her shoes, then went to the kitchen to make tea. As she passed the telephone, she saw that the red button was blinking. Samantha picked up the phone, punched in a four-digit code, then listened to Gray's voice.

"Sam. I just called out to California and discovered you were coming back. I then called Molly and Dan just minutes ago and discovered that you'd been here and had tried to call me. Guess where I was. I was at the house, no phone, painting. The back rooms are close to done and look great. Oh, one other thing, I'm on my way in to Boston. I'll see you soon."

Samantha smiled and held the phone at her neck. Then she wondered how she looked. She walked into the bathroom where she brushed her hair, then into her bedroom and changed from a tan jersey to a blouse in deep purple. With a touch of lipstick to her lips she felt ready to welcome Gray to her apartment, her arms, her life.

Within minutes of applying the lipstick, then blotting a bit of it off, there was a knock at her door. Samantha leaned her palms against the smooth surface and asked who was there.

"The big bad wolf," he said.

Samantha opened the door and, without hesitation, he walked in and claimed her with his hands around her waist and his lips to hers.

After several moments of their bodies swaying back and forth in a matching rhythm, Gray looked at Samantha and said, "I've missed you."

Samantha smiled and took his hand, leading him to the sofa. "Would you like something to drink? I have wine, coffee, tea, and soda."

"All I want is you," he said as he pulled her down next to him. "Don't go away on me again, Sam."

"It was something I needed to do," she said. "I'm glad I went; Kyle had issues getting around for a couple of weeks. But I missed you too. It put things in perspective for me though. I realized how much I wanted to leave Boston and move to Plymouth. I've been treading water in here for a few years now. Even though I love the museum, my work is writing the books and I want to concentrate on that."

"How about a little concentration on me?" he asked as he pulled her to him and kissed her again.

When he released her, he smiled. "It was worth every mile and minute coming here tonight. I had to see you."

"You aren't leaving yet, are you?"

"I should. I have a meeting early in the morning. But this weekend, are we doing the trip to Vermont?"

Samantha grimaced. "I don't know. Maybe not. I promised to get the children's room done in the museum. After this time, I'm through. And the lease on my apartment is up in a month and I'm packing it up. There's so much to do."

"When will I see you? If you can't get down to Plymouth, I'll come up here. We can do the North End again."

"How about if we see how the next couple of days go?"

"Okay. By the way, where's my cat?" Gray looked around the apartment from where he sat.

Samantha smiled. "Lucy is in Plymouth. She's content there.

So, when did she become *your* cat?"

"Oh, she's crazy about me," Gray said with a serious expression as he stood.

"I hate to see you go," she said as they walked toward the door.

Gray stopped with his hand on the door's handle. "I hate to see me go too," he said.

Ten minutes passed when the phone rang. Samantha smiled seeing Gray's cell phone number.

"Hi," she said.

"Hi," he said.

Samantha laughed. "Is that it? Just hi?"

"I'm happy having you on the other end of this phone and back within reach. I hated having you so far away in California."

"I know."

"Lucy didn't like it either."

Samantha laughed. "I'm sure."

"Yeah, well I'm sure you're tired. The flight from LA must have been a grind, and then your pesky boyfriend had to show up uninvited."

"Boyfriend? What boyfriend?"

"You'd better be kidding," he said. "Besides, Lucy wants me in her life."

Samantha smiled and sat down where he'd been sitting on her sofa.

"You there?" he asked.

"No," she said. "My heart is in Plymouth and my body is longing for bed."

"Gotcha," he said. "Go to bed, Sam. I'll talk to you soon."

"Okay. Goodnight, Gray."

She heard him murmur a whispered goodnight then she clicked off her phone and held it in both of her hands. Gray was comfortable. What had it been that Kate said when they visited Providence? Yes, it was that Paul made her feel she was home. Gray had that affect, home.

Chapter Fourteen

Over the next few days, Samantha spent from early morning until after eight at night at the museum organizing and directing the new displays for the children's room. She loved creating the vivid scenes, the animals dressed in colorful outfits, the lit stars she had arranged to be dangling from a lavender sky. Julie was delighted with the effect and all of the museum's employees and volunteers came to see the finished room.

"I can't believe you won't be here to do this anymore," Julie said. "Are you sure about this move, Samantha?"

"Yes," she said. "I'm sure."

Everything began to swirl into motion as her landlord told her that someone was moving in as soon as she moved out. Samantha worked late into several nights packing her belongings, organizing her boxes of books, her clothing, the accumulations she'd made just living in that space. The furniture wasn't something she cared about and it was offered for a fraction of the original cost to the new tenant. She would take bed linens and towels, but curtains, drapes, and large pieces would stay.

As she worked sorting through her personal belongings, making decisions on what to keep and what to discard, the phone rang. She picked it up expecting it to be Gray. Instead, she heard Will's raspy voice on the other end of the line.

"Will? You sound awful. What's the matter?"

"Oh, Sam, you don't want to know."

"Yes I do. What's going on?"

"I just got out of the hospital, pneumonia."

"What? How did you get pneumonia? Are you okay?"

"I'm here."

Samantha sighed. "Will, are you really okay? Where's your mother? Is she spoiling you with her chicken soup?"

"She's vacationing in Costa Rica."

Samantha took a deep breath.

"So, there's no one with you? You're on your own?"

"Yes. Completely. It's not so bad now; I'm just tired."

"This is awful. Someone should be there pampering you."

"That would be lovely. When are you coming?"

Samantha smiled. "Would you believe that I just got home from California less than a week ago? My brother, Kyle, was in an accident and needed help."

"Is he okay? Where are your parents at this point?"

"He's okay now. Mom and Dad are in Bali on the ship. But back to you, are you really in need of someone being there? I feel terrible that you're alone."

"I'd love a visit from you," he said. "There's an extra bedroom here, and you're more than welcome."

Samantha hesitated. The last thing she wanted to do was go away again, but Will was an old and dear friend. She called her grandparents and told them she was going. Molly was reluctant to give her advice but asked her if she was sure about this decision. Then she called Gray and left a message on his machine. She knew he'd understand and she'd be back as soon as possible.

With her apartment in order and ready for the move, Samantha boarded a plane for Chicago. From the airport to Will's place she took a bus; she could use his car while there.

"You are an angel in disguise," Will said when he opened his apartment door to her.

She hugged him and then urged him to go and sit down, and she would fix a meal with whatever she could find in the refrigerator. She would grocery shop later when she knew what was needed.

Eating a tasty creamed tuna on toast, Will watched Samantha sipping a cup of hot coffee.

"What's going on in your life? Tell me all about it."

Samantha smiled and looked away before looking back at her friend.

"It's kind of crazy. I quit the museum, I gave up my apartment, and I'm moving to Plymouth."

"Let me guess," Will said. "It's that hunk, what's his name? Gray?"

She nodded. "Yes, his name is Gray, but I'm moving to

Plymouth because I've realized that's where I should be. I love Boston, but I'm too alone there. Being at my grandparents' house made me realize how much I missed just hanging out with family."

"You're lucky," Will said. "I have my wander-lust mother, and I'm grateful for her, but I'd sure love to have the bonds you know. And what about this Gray guy? He's in the picture, right?"

Samantha smiled and blushed. "Yeah, he is."

"Serious?"

Samantha stood and walked to the kitchen where she left her coffee cup then she walked back to the dining area and sat across from Will. "It's not like we've talked about a commitment, but we're definitely interested in one another."

"In love?" Will asked. "Is my Samantha in love at last?"

Samantha laughed. "What do you mean at last? You make it sound like I'm fifteen or something."

Will gave her a stern look. "Who have you ever really cared about? Name me one guy."

Samantha sat back in her chair. "There was Jim."

"Come on, Sam. Jim was never a contender for your heart."

Samantha took Will's empty plate to the sink and washed it along with her coffee cup.

"So, this guy Gray, he's okay with you being here after just coming back from California?"

Samantha bit her bottom lip. "I don't know. I called and left him a message on his machine. The night I got back from LA, he drove up from Plymouth to Boston to see me for about ten minutes. He hated me being away. I was half-glad when he didn't answer the phone when I called to tell him I was leaving for Chicago."

"Good Lord, Samantha Elwyn! What kind of sabotage are you committing? What in the world are you doing here?"

"I came to see to you," she said defensively.

"Sam. Come on. You're getting cold feet, aren't you? Here's this terrific guy, wish he liked me, driving from Plymouth to Boston just to see you for ten minutes, and you're here with your gay friend. What the heck! Sam, go home!"

"I can't just turn around and leave you," she said.

Will stood up and walked around the table. "Yes, you can. See? I can walk, I can talk, I can do head-stands. Go home! I want to dance at your wedding. Who knows, maybe he's got a good looking gay friend who needs someone just like me and we'll hook up at the reception!"

Samantha smiled. "I'll call him later; he'll understand."

"Sam," Will said as he placed both of his hands on her forearms. "No, he won't. You're going to fool around and lose him, Sam. The man loves you. He wouldn't drive in to Boston just for the thrill of it. Go home, now."

Samantha began to feel an adrenalin surge as she thought about the possibility of losing Gray. That couldn't happen, or could it? Will was completely right. She was dragging her feet with this new experience, being afraid of being in love.

The plane ride back to Boston was too long, and as soon as she could climb into her car, she drove straight to Plymouth even though it was after ten at night. She drove past the house where his parents lived and saw that his car was not there. Could he be at his own home? She drove the mile to his house and saw his car parked in the driveway, lights were on in the house. She hesitated as she sat there wondering if he was going to welcome her or worry her. Finally Samantha stepped out of the car and walked to the front door. She knocked but no one answered. She used the key he'd given to her and called to him as she entered; there was no reply. She left her coat and purse on a chair and looked around, through the kitchen where there was a warm pot of coffee, and through the red room and finally toward the stairs. She walked up calling to him and he appeared from the back room with a paintbrush in his hand. The look on his handsome face was one that Samantha had not seen before. He looked injured.

"Gray," she said.

He turned and walked back into the room where he continued to paint. "I got your message," he said.

Samantha thought she might cry. Gray had never turned away from her before. "I'm sorry, Gray. I was an idiot to go off again. Will told me how stupid I was to be there with him when I could be here with you. I'm sorry."

Gray kept painting.

"Please, speak to me; tell me you're not furious with me."

He sighed. "Did you think I'd be okay with you going?"

"I didn't think at all," she said.

He was quiet as he painted long strokes of putty color on the walls.

"I was wondering," she said, "if we could take that trip to Vermont this coming weekend."

Gray turned and looked at her then placed the brush in a jar of water to soak.

"The only way I'm going to Vermont with you is if you agree to wearing this," he said as he pulled a small velvet box from his trouser pocket.

Samantha gasped for air as she stared at the beautiful diamond ring he revealed to her, and then she cried.

"Sam," he said as he placed one hand on each side of her face, "Don't. Don't ever go away again, don't cry, and don't say no to this ring."

"Okay," she said.

"You'll accept the ring? That means you're mine you know. No more anyone else. Mine."

"Okay."

"I finished painting the room," he said.

"Okay," she said in return.

"I want to tackle the blue room, the Wedgewood room next," he said.

"Okay," she agreed.

"We're on a roll here," he said as he wiped away her tears and kissed her lightly. "So, you'll marry me and we'll live in this great old house together forever after."

"Okay," she said.

Molly's Maple Cake

In a large bowl combine:
3 Cups of Flour
2 And ½ Cups of Sugar
½ Tsp. Salt
2 Level Tsps. Baking Powder
Mix dry ingredients together well.

Add:
1 Cup Soft or Melted Margarine or Butter
3 Eggs
3 Tsps. Maple Flavoring
½ Cup Water or Milk

Mixture will be thick – Bake at 350 for about thirty minutes – test with a toothpick or cake tester in the center of the cake. This batter will make three nice layers (which is what Molly made for Thanksgiving), or 1 large 9"x13" cake.

Frosting:

Combine
3 Cups of Confectioners' Sugar
½ Cup Melted Butter or Margarine
3 Tsps. Maple Flavoring

Add:
Cream or Milk, 1 teaspoon at a time, until you have the desired consistency to frost your cake.

You may also wish to garnish the cake with walnuts or pecans.

www.ingramcontent.com/pod-product-compliance
Lightning Source LLC
Chambersburg PA
CBHW070923130626

46555CB00001B/265